THE LOST
SCRIBE

THE LOST
SCRIBE

FORGOTTEN CHANNEL OF THE ANCIENTS

By

AMY GILLESPIE

ISBN: 978-0-692-10411-8

Written by AMY GILLESPIE
www.amygillespie.com

Edits by CHERI COLBURN
chericolburn@gmail.com
Linkedin/in/cheri-colburn

Cover Design by Mario Lampic
Author Photo taken by Simone Severo
Design Layout by Zora Knauf

Website: http://www.amygillespie.com

Illumination Station

For the children.

And for those who keep them safe.

CONTENTS

PREFACE

When I received the following message, the first Maddie Clare Owens book had already been written in my mind. Many of the experiences woven into these pages had already occurred, and the messages had already been received, written, and dated.

"Find the frequency, Dear One. Find it, hold it, recognize it, love it, and stabilize it so you can hold it for longer and longer periods of time. Come to a space where you yearn and ache to reach the octave—can hardly wait to reach the octave—each day. Then your gifts will truly flower. This is your goal, your Destiny."
~ Melchizedek, October 6, 2014

That same year, my channeling referenced an undiscovered tomb within a pyramid, but I did not share that information with the world. I simply could not fathom that the messages could be real.

Repeatedly, I was called to share the messages with the world, and by 2016, I was actively seeking a sacred location and a sacred symbol for this first story. That's when I accepted a chance invitation to a friend's wedding in Cancun. On that trip, many things came together, as you will read in these pages. As I approached the great pyramid of El Castillo, the familiarity of the barred door (which I had seen in earlier visions) was undeniable. The location for the story was chosen for me by the Universe.

Not long after that trip, the chamber within El Castillo was discovered. If I had shared that knowledge when I received it—in 2014, if I had not resisted the writing of this book…the premonitory nature of the visions would have been virtually undeniable. I take all of that as a little spanking from the Universe to publish my books on time.

ACKNOWLEDGEMENTS

Where do I begin to thank everyone who has supported me on this journey? First is God—because God brought each of you into my life in a certain "Divine Order." I am blessed every moment of every day by the angelic messages and Divine support I receive.

Thank you to my beloved Daniel—my greatest surprise in love and life. His support and words helped me craft my journal messages, childhood and adult visions, and actual experiences into the folds of a fiction novel. His creativity allowed me to weave this tale into reality.

Huge thanks to my most amazing editor, Cheri Colburn. This book would not be in your hands if it weren't for her work, sorting out my fumbled chapters and disorganized notes. She helped my story come through in a way that will make you want to read the next page, the next chapter—maybe even the next book. Her resilience and drive are an amazing gift to any author struggling to get a book "out of their head and into their hands." Thank you, Cheri.

I thank my family (especially my parents) for their patience, for their resilience, for putting up with me, the oddity in the family who went around the globe, chasing whispers; who now is turning her "whispers" into the Maddie Clare Owens (MCO) Adventure Series.

This book would not be complete, save for the input of each of my amazing review team, gifting their viewpoints to this first MCO book from their personal perspectives. Chosen like a great team of jurors, they were picked for their very unique and distinctive life journeys to mold this story into one that can reach a greater audience. Thank you, MacKenzie, Lorée, Micki, Dan, Amanda, and Cindy.

Most of all, I thank you—the reader—for taking the chance on buying this book and its wild weave of real and surreal. I hope it changes your life, as it has mine.

I wish you a very blessed journey~

THE LOST
SCRIBE

NESCIENCE

PROLOGUE

Brief moments of silence were interspersed with the sound of the carbon-black gliding across the codex. Folded pages of bark were stretched out across the cool stone table, and she had reached the final page. The words appeared as quickly as her young hands would allow. She had to finish the codex.

Trembling slightly, she carefully dipped the quill pen into the ink. She needed to get the last bit of information exactly right. There would be no time to correct an error.

The stone room was temperate and luminescent, designed for the uniform drying of the ink. She glanced at the twelve scrolls already stacked at the end of the stone masonry, each with its own seal, indicating the scribe who had created them. The scrolls were the final works of priests and priestesses murdered by the men in steel hats, men who had come from the sea, riding in on four-legged beasts.

Her own scroll was there, too. She was the only one who remained of the priests, priestesses, and other scribes who had accepted this grave endeavor. She wondered if she would face the same demise.

She needed to finish the last few lines of the codex, sacred messages that were to be hidden away for millennia. Pausing for just a moment, she remembered the head priest's intent gaze as he gave her the final directive. "It's up to you Naats' sayab. You are the last of us. I will lead the Spaniards into the jungle, so you have time to finish my codex and get it to the depository, with the other scrolls. Wrap it in the jaguar skin and place it behind the stones, with the others.

"As we have seen in the long count and the stars, the codices must not be discovered before the year 2020. That is the year of structure, of building the foundation of the future. These messages must only be revealed in that year. It is the way of the Universe. You have been taught well to complete this charge."

Her hands had trembled at the enormity of the task. In an act of unusual warmth, the priest had taken her hands into his own. "Do not fear your own weaknesses. This assignment has come from the Universe. This act has been written since the beginning of the long count, more than one million days ago. You cannot fail. It is impossible to alter the trajectory of what we have been called to do. You will not fail."

She took a deep breath and swept her hair side to side across her shoulders. Suddenly, the white tunic felt cumbersome, too big for her slight body.

"There should be more sacred ceremony for this."

"In that you are correct," the priest said, looking down at her fondly, "but there is no time. They are so close; you can hear the screaming. I must go now. We will meet in another life. Remember to hide my codex inside your tunic. You will be able to pass the Spaniards unnoticed.

"Put my codex in the secret place and take the others to the Temple of the Jaguars to be watched over by Ah Muzem Cab. Those who come behind us will keep it safe, together with the scrolls. The Universe, herself, will keep them secret until their intended time, just as we have all been guided day by day to reach this moment.

As he stood in the doorway, the great priest glanced back to her over his shoulder. "Naats' sayab, do not let self-doubt overtake you. You are more than you think, more than you remember." With that, the priest disappeared to the great stairway, leaving her in silence to finish her formidable task.

PART I:

THE NEOPHYTE

CHAPTER 1

At the slap of the muddy hand on her back, she shrieked and pitched herself sharply to the right, managing to slip his grasp. She slid and skittered on the wet jungle surface, tripping on a craggy tree root, and her tiny, half-naked body tumbled to the ground. She dove through a small opening underneath a fallen tree and gained some advantage over her much-larger pursuer. Still hearing the trampling feet of the attackers on the jungle floor, she scuttled back to her feet and ran on.

Fueled by terrified screams of the other children, she surged forward over vines and wet leaves, while branches scratched at her face and body. Sweat poured down her face, stinging the fresh abrasions, and jagged jungle branches tore at the cloth about her waist, all that was left of her clothing she had worn to work in the fields.

Breathlessly gasping, she looked up and saw a glimmer of light through the now-thinning jungle foliage. She was approaching the clearing. If she made it there, she might be okay. *They* could not step into the light.

She burst out of the jungle, the blinding sun nearly stopping her, but she could still hear the heavy trampling on the path behind her. She stumbled forward.

When she regained her footing, she stole a look back. She didn't see any other children, and she no longer heard their screams. Maddie Clare assumed they had each fallen to their captors. The mud-covered faces behind her revealed triumph, even though she had escaped. Then she felt the ground giving way and spun back around to see … nothing. She tried to stop, tried to catch her balance on the edge of the cliff.

Then there was only the sensation of falling. The world went silent.

* * *

The sound of the doorbell sent Maddie straight out of her chair, spilling her glass of wine. She trembled and gasped for air, trying to come back to the present moment. She raced down the steps to her door, while her Basset hound, Maybelle, licked up the mess.

A large envelope fell at her feet as she opened the door. In the street, the FedEx truck was pulling away.

With a forceful exhale, she released some of her inner chaos and picked up the envelope, addressed to Miss Maddie Clare Owens. She tugged at the pull string of the envelope as she headed back up the stairs to clean up the wine, which was undoubtedly soaking into her chair.

At the top of the steps she pulled out the contents, and noticed the post-it on the front, "In case you decide to come! Love, Jessica and Andrew." She thumbed open the cover of the booklet to *Grand Oasis Tulum, February 2016.* Clearing a dry spot on the coffee table for the package, she strolled to the kitchen for a rag. She blotted the stain with a towel and noticed the wine had only darkened her colorful upholstery.

There were red specks on Maybelle's white chest. "You missed a spot, Sweetie. Tough to reach, eh?" Smiling, she leaned down and toweled off the wine. Then she checked the stain on the chair one last time. Satisfied she'd gotten it all, she sat on the edge of the coffee table and took deep breaths to calm down.

Tilting her head from side to side, she swung her loose hair behind her. This nightmare came night after night, always the same—just as the equally vivid nightmares had come to her, again and again, when she was eleven years old.

The first nightmares had changed her entire life, and now she couldn't shake the feeling of déjà vu. The events in the dreams were nearly identical, but more important, she once again had the sense that *something* was about to change forever.

For years before the childhood nightmares, she had indulged in a fantasy world of "visions." That's what Grandma Cora had called them. According to Grandma, they weren't dreams because they only came when she was awake. In Maddie's final conversation with her grandmother, Cora had told Maddie Clare, "Hold the visions close to your heart, like a great secret. Not everyone will understand your gift."

So that is what Maddie Clare had done. She kept the visions secret. To her, they were a magic, hidden pleasure, often indulged.

To summon the visions, Maddie only had to lie awake and relax, with her eyes gently closed. The visions would simply begin. Just like dreams in the night, she never knew what she would see. But unlike dreams, in the visions she hovered over the scene and looked down from above.

Many of her visions included rooms filled with mysterious instruments she couldn't name. Later, she learned they were sextants, geological equipment, surveying tools, and scientific measuring tools of every variety. She saw people she didn't recognize, who wore antiquated clothing. They would appear and linger for a moment before the next image came.

The people reminded her of the old-fashioned immigrants she had seen in photographs at her grandma's house, and she wondered if she'd made them up from those photos. Other times, she wondered if the images were fragments of old television shows. But the images were so elaborate and so unfamiliar, she couldn't believe she created them herself.

The visions were an endless source of mystery to her, but aside from very early conversations with her grandma, she never spoke about them with the adults in her life. She was confident her parents would rationalize her fantastical world, and she didn't think she could bear it. In her mind, she heard her mother's pragmatic voice saying, "Now Maddie Clare, you know that just isn't possible." She couldn't bear that. The visions were too precious to her.

By the time she was eight, the barns had become her favorite hideaway to enjoy her secret. She would nestle into the straw at the back of the hayloft and make herself comfortable. Then, while listening to the Nebraska winds wail through long-broken windowpanes, she simply allowed the visions to come. The only effort she had to make was to keep her active brain from getting involved. If she tried to probe the scenes, seeking details, oftentimes the visions would dissolve, and the experience would end.

As she got better at summoning the visions, they changed. Grayscale images were replaced with full color. She saw people talking, dancing, having meetings, and chatting on telephones. The images were fascinating but incomprehensible. Without exception, they were silent. This one thing never changed—in the early years.

Over time, the images became more complex, and her ability to manipulate them grew. By the time she was nine, she found she could use the visions to find answers to everyday questions. One time her father was late coming home from the fields, and she wondered where he was. She simply tipped her head back and began to think of him. She imagined the crunch of his tires in the driveway and the way he looked walking in the door. Immediately, she saw him in her mind, visiting their friends Harvey and Norma, surrounded by puppies.

Sure enough, when he got home, he told her and her brother that Harvey and Norma had a new litter of pups. Even more significant to Maddie, her dad was wearing the exact clothes she had seen in her vision, although she hadn't seen him earlier that day. The experience made quite an impression. Her grandma was right. The visions were truly a gift.

Her new ability allowed her to use the visions to finish any dream from which she'd awakened—and sometimes to control the outcome. When completing a dream with a vision, Maddie could even bring in sounds and scents, as if the vision were a real-life experience. In one dream, she and her best friend Lynda, dressed as warriors with large swords, were defending a dark building. Lynda cried out, and Maddie woke up.

She couldn't go back to sleep, so she summoned a vision. Lynda and Maddie were battling with nine male warriors. Lynda was at the top of the stairs, the last guardian at the gate, and Maddie was at the bottom of the stairs, in full battle. Finally, when the last man was beaten, Lynda and Maddie returned to their positions, one on each side of the gate.

An older woman appeared and, in a resonant, otherworldly voice, told them they had done well in guarding the 12th gate. This had been their mission.

Maddie hadn't thought of those early visions, nor her heightened ability to use them, for a long time. She didn't know at the time how pristine and innocent they were.

Then the nightmares came.

With that thought, Maddie Clare drained the last droplets of wine from her glass.

When she was about 11, she started to have terrifying dreams. In some, she was being chased. In others, she was trapped within cold, stone walls. Always, she was surrounded by the screams of young children. Unlike the visions, which she saw from above, the nightmares put her in the thick of the action, feeling abject terror as she ran through the woods or groped dark, ice-cold walls. Like tonight.

Her childhood chase nightmare was similar to the one she'd been having recently. She was running through a jungle with other terrified children. Now and again, a child would be snatched up by an unseen predator. Just like in tonight's dream, she would burst into the clearing and find herself teetering on a precipice, a deep rocky well below.

Why is this happening again? What provoked the return of those nightmares?

In the childhood nightmare, Maddie had turned around to face twenty men with black hair and dark, piercing eyes. At that point, the other children were gone, and she alone was left to face them. From head to toe, they were smeared in mud, with twigs and branches clinging to their chests, arms, and legs. As she stared back at them, she could see more of them in the forest, camouflaged against the trees. To her, they became the *mud people*.

Every effort she made to use a vision to finish that nightmare ended with the mud people pushing her child-body off the cliff. Absolutely certain that she was going to die at the bottom, Maddie always opened her eyes the moment she felt herself slipping.

Maddie couldn't understand why that nightmare was different, why she couldn't control it. She thought maybe that nightmare was replaying—or foretelling—a real event.

Maddie Clare became frightened of the visions for the first time in her life. She worried that they might be premonitions. Even at 11, she understood the burden of being able to see something before it actually happened. What if she asked some question and received an awful—or even terrifying—vision? What if she told people something was going to happen and it didn't? They would call her a liar, at best. Suddenly, the weight of the visions replaced her earlier playtime perspective.

With the arrival of the nightmares and the disquieting thought that they could be pre-cognitive, Maddie swore her gift away, promising herself never again to access the other world. She stopped visiting the sanctuary of the hayloft, and each time she felt herself easing into a vision, she shook her long dark hair behind her, like a flounce. That simple motion cleared any vision nearly as quickly as it had begun.

About a month after the first mud-people nightmare, Maddie Clare got her first menstrual cycle, and the nightmares stopped. So did the visions. She never knew if it was due to her maturing body or her own will, but it was over, and she was glad. She never told anyone, and for many years, she didn't try to access the supernatural.

Contemplating that difficult time made Maddie even more apprehensive about the return of the nightmares. The mud people still terrified her, and in one disturbing way, her current nightmares were even worse than the ones before. She was a child in both dreams and frightened when she awoke, but now the dreams left her with the additional urge to find—and help—the other screaming children. Her concern for those children followed her as she went about her daily life. She was constantly looking for signs that they might be real children needing help, trying to get her attention through the nightmares.

She thrust herself up and headed toward the kitchen.

I need a drink!

Stopping in the bathroom long enough to rinse her hands and soak the wine-stained towel in soapy water, Maddie glanced in the mirror. Sweeping bangs framed her ivory skin and high cheekbones, setting off her heterochromatic eyes. Giving her body's reflection a sidelong glance, she put her hand to her hip, "I've got to get back into the size eights. Hourglass or no, a ten is too big for my height."

Maddie passed the hall desk and noticed her computer screen flashing, nagging her to Buy Now.

Strange the computer screen didn't go to sleep. Must be a sign.

Her thumb traced the cool, smooth edge of the mouse-pad as she stared at the screen. Buy Now taunted her.

Should I do it? A thousand bucks!

She pursed her lips back and forth and tapped the edge of the keypad, willing the answer to come. She knew she'd feel awkward—like a fifth wheel—as "the friend of the bride's Mom." But still …

It might be just the thing.

Her eyes searched the heavens for the answer.

Oh, what to do …

She stretched, reaching to the sky and shaking her hair loose behind her.

Just click it, Maddie Clare!

She exhaled forcefully and heeded the Buy Now command. She filled in her billing details and selected Yes for $29.95 flight insurance.

Not much for peace of mind.

When it was done, the firm feeling of resolve in her belly told her she'd made the right choice.

This should give the Universe a chance to get me out of this rut. Maybe it will even shake loose these crazy nightmares.

Once she confirmed a receipt had landed in her email, she flipped to her iTunes and found Bob Seger's "Turn the Page." The sultry verses began, and she got up from the table to stretch her arms high and wide, arching her back right then left. Shrugging her shoulders, she continued her journey to the kitchen.

It's after dark, almost eight-thirty. Definitely time for more wine.

She filled her glass, and then wrapped her arm around Maybelle. "How about you, girl? Will you be okay with the doggy sitter while I seek love, fame, and fortune in Cancun?"

The chubby pooch looked up at her with sad eyes—sad, Basset-hound eyes—the very saddest eyes in the dog world as far as Maddie was concerned. Maddie noted a still-pink spot on Maybelle's chest.

Maybe she's not sad, but just a bit drunk.

She reached down, grabbed Maybelle's long, flowing ears, and gave them a good shake. "Don't be sad, little girl. You will still get your treats. Eh?" Maybelle shook her head, maybe because she didn't like having her ears played with or maybe to shake off the tension that had been hovering in the air. Maddie Clare headed back toward the chair.

Oh my God! I'm going to Cancun ... an all-inclusive, beach-side resort at Riviera Maya! A virtual cruise ship on land!

She did a little Irish-jig happy-dance and dropped back into the chair, throwing her legs over the side. Tipping her glass back and forth, she watched the Cabernet's legs stream down one side and then the other. She continued to swirl the glass slowly as she leaned back and closed her eyes.

Seeing Kenny and Lynda, and their three daughters, might be just the thing to shift Maddie's energy. Lynda was one of Maddie's oldest friends, and they had hit it off from the start. They were natural soul-sisters, who stayed close from the fourth grade, when they met, all through school. Years later, Maddie was honored when Lynda asked her to be MacKenzie's godmother.

A year or two into her friendship with Lynda, she had almost ignored her grandmother's advice and told Lynda about her visions. But just as she was considering the possibility, the nightmares had started, and her fear tainted the visions. For the first time, they weren't Maddie's precious gift; instead they were something slightly menacing. The idea of talking about them made it feel more frightening, not less.

Maddie had been raised Catholic, and Lynda was Baptist. As teenagers, they had gone to each other's churches to see what the "other side" was like. Lynda had gone on for days about what an aerobic experience Catholic mass was, with sitting, kneeling, and standing. "When do you guys pray in humble silence like the rest of the world? And where the heck are the Bibles? And why is it so dark?" Maddie couldn't argue with Lynda's points of view. In some sense, she was glad to have someone make light of the spiritual side of life. Sometimes it all felt a little too heavy, a little too real for Maddie.

Finally back in the present moment, Maddie reached for the envelope. It was from Lynda's daughter, Jessica, the bride-to-be. "Well, that's a coincidence, isn't it, Maybelle?"

Maddie picked up the little pamphlet from Jessica and smiled as she opened the cover. It was all about the upcoming wedding, with a page telling a bit about each guest, how Jessica and Andrew knew them, and what role the person played in the couple's life. Maddie was glad to have it. Aside from correspondence and an occasional phone call with her goddaughter, Maddie had mostly lost touch with Lynda's girls. She barely knew Jessica, the bride, or her older sister Dani. Beyond names, she didn't know anything about the groom, Andrew, nor Dani's husband, Reed.

The booklet was a nice touch for a destination wedding, like an ice-breaker. There were pages dedicated to the hotel, the local markets, travel FAQ's, and some available tours in the area. The complete four-day schedule was in there, from bachelorette party on Thursday night to a special trip to the Maya ruins of Tulum on Monday.

An archaeological adventure! If I hadn't already decided, I would surely go after this! Woo-hoo!

With that, Maddie put the booklet back in the Fed Ex envelope, taking it to her bedroom to tuck into her carryon. While she was there, she grabbed her journal. Then she returned to the tilt-a-whirl chair, swinging her legs over the side.

When Maddie was a little girl, her mother had given her a diary. She had never been the consistent diarist her mother wanted her to be, but she enjoyed it. Maybe that's why, when she heard about automatic writing in her early 20s, it seemed a perfectly natural idea. She thought it might be a safe way to get back the guidance she'd missed for so long. Time had confirmed that theory, and Maddie enjoyed the guidance she perceived came from automatic writing.

She always began her sessions the same way, with the date and the first line, "My Dear and Loving Angels and Guides, speak to me as you will ..." She would hold the pen loosely, writing whatever message came to mind and crediting the ideas to the angels and her spiritual sponsors. She never knew for sure whether any of it was real, but she felt strongly that much of the information could not have come from her own thoughts. It was too otherworldly. Some entries included symbols and the names of things she didn't yet understand, just as the visions had included faces and geological equipment she couldn't identify at the time.

Maddie recalled how it had been to finally see the real-world equipment, during her college days at the University of Minnesota. She felt a surge of excitement the first time she saw a sextant that was exactly what she had seen in her earliest vision. Soon, passing the college labs became a new pastime, pressing her nose to the glass to see if she could identify anything else she had seen in her early years. Whenever she had the opportunity, she took a long, deep look at each item, absorbed by details she could never scrutinize in the vision-state.

Seeing the equipment provided silent confirmation that she had seen real things. She started to suspect that if the scientific things had been real, perhaps the people and events were real, too. Only her memory of the nightmares—the terrifying mud people—and her fear that they, too, might be real, kept her from reopening the channel to see the visions again. If real children were being murdered somewhere in a real jungle, she couldn't bear to know it.

She had begun college, like most students, with excitement and optimism. And she loved her studies!

So, Maddie threw herself into her schooling. She reveled in her freshman and early sophomore years, learning so much about the world and about herself. She had settled on archaeology as a major. She viewed archaeology as a hunt for ancient treasures, and she knew it would be the perfect career for her. She vowed to get her required courses out of the way quickly, so she could really dive into archeological study and maybe even go on a dig.

Then, late in her sophomore year, she began to struggle with her finances. When a recruiter at a job fair took an interest in her, she accepted a job as an insurance adjuster, *just for the summer*. Twenty years later she had a solid reputation as *the* adjuster for specialty research and complex claims.

Maddie sighed. She couldn't help but wonder how different her life would have been if she had continued her studies of ancient cultures. The thought inspired her to empty her wineglass.

Maybe one more before bed, just to fend off the screams. After all, I did spill half of the first one.

Maddie filled her glass and returned to her "comfy chair." That's what everybody called it, instantly, upon sitting down. She had purchased the chair not long after moving to Colorado, by responding to an ad. Not only did she get some great furniture, she met her first Colorado friend, Ruth.

Maddie's friendship with Ruth reminded her of her connection with Lynda. Ruth, too, felt something like a soul-sister, though their life experiences had been very different. Ruth had once enjoyed a career in the Air Force and was the mother of two children. While Maddie wasn't quite sure what to make of psychics, but Ruth was a practicing psychic and a Puerto Rican shaman. In fact, she traveled to Puerto Rico every year to serve on a high council.

They'd had a number of light-hearted discussions in which Ruth made predictions about Maddie's future. Maddie recalled one of the recent messages, which (Maddie had thought) began with a typically broad, vague statement. "You will be going on a long journey …"

"This will be a journey with many gates—small, brightly colored gates. They will be difficult to fit through." With that, Ruth had gone to her bookshelf and pulled down two books, *Opening to Channel* and *The Intuitive Way*. Placing them in Maddie's hands, she only said, "For your journey." That was three weeks ago, and the books were still sitting on the hall table.

Still, the titles had given Maddie the hope that as she got to know Ruth, she might be able to tell her about her supernatural experiences. Already Maddie could tell Ruth wouldn't mock her or make light of spiritual or even supernatural experiences. She had even wondered if the books were Ruth's way of inviting the conversation, as if to tell Maddie Clare she already knew her secret.

Maybe after Cancun ...

Aside from Ruth's furniture, Maddie's apartment wasn't anything special. The staircase entry gave it a lovely loft feeling, but nearly every other aspect of the place—especially the 1970s paneling—was dingy and drab. Maddie was grateful she'd taken only a six-month lease, just enough time to get acclimated to Colorado.

"When I get back from Cancun, we'll make a fresh start," she said to Maybelle. "I'll find you a proper house with a yard, so you can run around."

Maybe I'll even give up the wine—or at least slow to a normal pace.

Like her parents, Maddie Clare didn't necessarily frown on alcohol. She had just never been big on it. It seemed a silly expense—of money, time, and potential. She knew that if she was going to make a meaningful contribution in the world, the drinking would have to slow down or stop. With that thought, she gulped down the last mouthful of wine.

After Cancun ... Cancun.

The word seemed mystical to Maddie. It beckoned, and she vaguely wondered if it was like a Siren's song beckoning sailors onto the rocks.

The foggy buzz from the wine made it easy to leave the journal on the table as she headed for bed.

No prophesies tonight, please. I'm tired.

Once in her bedroom, Maddie noticed her air mattress was starting to go flat. She intended—after

Cancun—to find a home that would accommodate a queen-sized bed. But this arrangement hadn't been too bad. It gave Maybelle easy access to snuggle. Chubby Maybelle, at 70 pounds, would never get on a "real" bed by herself.

Maddie changed into her yoga pants (which had never seen a yoga studio) and crawled into bed. She pulled the comforter closer and felt Maybelle's full weight wiggling into a backward spoon against her body.

All snuggled in.

With an image of Cancun lingering in her mind, she said her normal evening prayer.

> *"God, Angels, and all of my spiritual sponsors, lead me to my dreams. Show me what is most important for me to know and wake me to remember what's important in the morning.*
>
> *Oh, but—please—no screaming children. No screaming anything! Goodnight."*

Sometimes Maddie felt odd saying *goodnight* instead of *amen*. But *goodnight* conveyed a family feeling, the true proximity she felt with the Divine.

She snuggled deeper into the mattress, thinking again that she'd better add some air. Maybelle, apparently, felt just right. She sighed, long and deep, sounding every bit as human as any human could.

"Goodnight, Maybelle."

CHAPTER 2

Maddie's excitement grew as the weeks passed. The nightmares continued, but she managed to bustle about her work and to enjoy the holidays, during which she told everyone about her upcoming adventure. Friends and family were more than happy to mention things they would love to get from Mexico, and Maddie had a reputation for always picking the perfect gift. The pressure was on.

Finally on her way to the airport, she reviewed her gift list. Her wallet was still thin from holiday shopping, and she was a bit concerned.

Who gets married right after Christmas?

Maddie stowed her bag under the seat and settled in to enjoy five hours of sleep on the overnight flight. The woman next to her said, "You're so lucky to have the window. Have you ever flown during a full moon? On the water below, every wave will have a silver shimmer. You'll never see it anywhere else. It's amazing."

Maddie looked out the window expectantly but found only a dark and cloudy night. She turned back to her seatmate. "Oh, thanks. Hopefully we will break through the clouds and I can see it."

A familiar buzz, from the wine she had drunk at the airport bar, began to take over. She lifted a foot to the back of the armrest in front of her and pulled herself close to the window. Leaning her head against the cool bulkhead, she silently whispered her bedtime prayer, ending with, "Wake me for the full moon, please." She laid a sweater across her lap and fell asleep before the cabin lights were turned down.

About an hour into the flight, she felt a chill, but it had nothing to do with the temperature of the plane's cabin. She was in the nightmare. She shivered as she placed her hand on the cold wall, and though the surface was cool, a bead of sweat dropped from her brow. Her hands stretched out to feel cold, cold walls in the dark.

She felt her way along what she imagined to be a hallway until she came to a break in the stone—a door. One gentle press, and the door silently opened. The room she entered was filled with a soft glow, and she could see a slender figure with shoulder-length black hair hunching over a stone table. Maddie Clare took a deep breath as she prepared to announce herself.

Then, from outside the walls, she heard a blood-curdling scream. She jumped back and again found herself alone in complete darkness. The room and the mysterious figure had disappeared. She groped the cold flat stones but couldn't find an opening. The single scream multiplied. Many terrified children were shrieking on the other side of the stones.

She had the urge to run, but toward what? To the screams? Away from the screams? Her disorientation was complete. There was no way to identify direction in the abyss, except that the floor was under her.

The children seemed to go silent, one by one. Certain she could save the remaining children if she could just find them, she clawed her way down the walls, finally seeing a crack of light ahead. She rushed to the door, crying out, "No!"

Maddie jolted upright, and her foot fell from the seat in front of her. She looked around to determine if she had yelled out loud. Nobody stirred. The man across the aisle continued to work on his laptop. She assumed she had kept the nightmare to herself and gave a brief sigh of relief.

Remembering the moon, Maddie looked out. An indigo sky was a backdrop for a full moon whose rays danced across the shoreline. Silvery reflections on the water left her with a feeling of awe and great anticipation for what was to come.

Then she noticed a perfect spotlight on the rocky beach. She tried to determine whether it was a light from the plane or the moon. The spotlight slid along the beach and rocky shore in perfect pace with the plane, as if she were shining a spotlight from her very own airplane window.

Who knew the moon could make a perfect spotlight? Was it an effect from the ocean? From her height in the sky?

She felt incredibly lucky at having chosen this side of the plane, where she could now clearly see every home, structure, tree, and beach magically illuminated by the full moon. As the sun started to peek above the horizon, Maddie drifted back to sleep.

Not long after, she was awakened by the pilot's morning announcement to see the magical night had been replaced by the grayish hue of dawn. The excited energy of the passengers was contagious, and Maddie imagined the adventures awaiting her in Cancun. When the plane pulled into the gate, she stood to stretch and gave thanks that she was short enough to do so.

She shifted her legs back and forth and leaned down to look out the window once more. Her mouth expressed a little pout that the magical scene of the full moon had been replaced with airplane tugs and cargo vans on the tarmac. Still, she couldn't contain her excitement at arriving.

Woo-hoo! I'm in Cancun!

She waggled her shoulders back and forth in a little happy-dance, glancing around to see if anyone noticed. Nobody did, not that she could see. The aisleway was clearing, and people were exiting the plane.

As she disembarked, she laughed, realizing she had expected to see people in brightly colored clothes and sombreros. Instead, she saw people in business clothes that far outclassed her blue jeans and knit top. As she passed by the still-closed, steel-gated shops, colorful bags and scarves caught her eye.

When she reached the front of the customs line, a young man beckoned her to his window, and she handed him her passport.

"How long will you be staying, Miss Owens?"

"Just a long weekend. For a wedding."

"Ah. Family?" He eyed her directly.

Does he think I am lying? Smuggling drugs? Carrying something illegal?

"My best friend's daughter," she mumbled.

Dang! I hope I don't have to repeat that awkward explanation over and over again—"the friend of the bride's mother."

His brow wrinkled, and he looked at her a bit more closely. Then he jutted his index finger at the passport. Ah, Miss Owens, it says here your eyes are blue."

"Oh. Yes. One of them is." She laughed, glad for the distraction. Opening her eyes wide for him to examine, she handed him her driver's license. "See? BR-BL. That's for brown and blue."

"Ah. Very good, señora. They are very beautiful—a very unique feature. I have never seen eyes like yours, and I see a lot of people." He looked at her with warm appreciation.

"Thanks," she smiled, "I read the odds are something like one in ten thousand to have two different colored eyes, so I guess I'm lucky. And lucky to be in your beautiful country."

"Enjoy your stay here. You must visit our Maya temples. They hold great history and beauty."

"I'm already scheduled to visit Tulum. Thank you, sir."

The slam of the stamp on her passport punctuated their conversation, and she moved on.

When Maddie exited to the waiting area, she was met by about ten hungry-looking taxi drivers. None held a placard with her name. She felt a little silly expecting it, but Lynda had said there would be a taxi waiting for her.

Now what?

She'd heard her share of horror stories about traveling south of the border, which made her leery. The last thing she needed was to start her trip with an insanely expensive taxi ride.

A heavy-set man in his thirties approached her. "Are you needing a taxi, señora?"

Trying to sound confident, she said, "No, sir. I'm headed to the Grand Oasis Tulum. There's a taxi waiting for me."

"Ah yes," he said, pointing, "outside that door."

Her expression must have revealed her suspicion. He walked out the door and promptly returned with another man, who wore a light-blue uniform shirt that said, "Grand Oasis Tulum."

Well, that was kind.

Maddie beamed at the man who had found her driver. "Thank you, sir!"

The first man bowed his head gallantly, and the new driver pulled out a clipboard. Looking down, he asked, "Maddie Clare Owens?"

"Yes. That's me. Is it far to the hotel?"

"About three hours," he said, as he picked up her bag and walked out. She followed dutifully, her carryon slung over her shoulder.

"If you like, Miss Owens, we can stop at the market in the city, where souvenirs are less expensive than they are closer to the beach. The stop adds nothing to the trip fee."

"Sure," Maddie said, "sounds great."

She climbed into the van, thinking, *Isn't that clever? They probably do a little side business, getting commissions from vendors and better tips from tourists. Smart. I like this guy!*

The sky had turned pale blue, announcing the coming sunrise, but it didn't matter to Maddie Clare. She was about to take a nice, long nap. The full-moon red-eye had been a beautiful flight, but in her mind and body, this time of day was for sleeping. She set her bag at her feet and hooked her seatbelt loosely. Within minutes, she was asleep on the bench seat behind the driver, trusting he had everything under control.

Next thing Maddie knew, she was waking to ba-bump, ba-bump. She lifted her head to see what was happening.

"Sorry, señora. The road to the market has some speed bumps."

She sat up and finger-combed her hair, while she took in the strange sights and sounds of the market.

As if reading her mind, the taxi driver said, "I suggest I go with you to translate. Your things will be safe in the van." Then he pointed. "We will go there."

Maddie saw only a cement structure with open doorways and a sign stenciled on the wall—Mercado 28.

"We can go inside, where private vendors will show you unique gifts. That is where you find the deals. Once you get to the hotel the prices go up."

"I understand, but I'll only get a couple things today, as I've just arrived."

"Of course, señora. After this, you will know which prices are fair and how to work the negotiating if you go to another market."

"Well, that is very nice of you."

He flashed a toothy smile. "Shall we go?"

Maddie put on a touch of lip gloss. "Onward!"

She didn't wait for him to open the door but pushed her bag under the front seat, grabbed her purse, and stepped out. He led her down a few steps into a tight maze of rich colors. She looked down the aisles and saw booth after booth of concessioners. She realized how easy it would be to get lost, and she was glad to have her escort.

They passed leather works, candles, woven baskets, and clothing. They passed food and candies, sombreros and rugs. At each doorway, people with jet black hair and brown eyes greeted them, smiling warmly and promising a good deal. Maddie was breathless with sensory overload.

This market has every single beautiful thing. I wish I'd brought an extra suitcase.

"You let me know if you see anything you like, Miss Maddie Clare. Is there something special you are looking for? Maybe clothing? Or leather? We have wonderful leather craftsmen. Also beautiful pottery, hand-painted."

The courtyard opened into an atrium of more shops, with little trees and benches in the center. Most vendors were housed in white shops trimmed with colorful storefronts, but a few walked around, carrying their wares on their arms.

As they came around a corner, Maddie Clare noticed an older woman with gold-rimmed front teeth and a big warm smile. She had a long gray braid that reached her skirt. The woman stepped forward as if to pull Maddie toward her.

Oh! I want to meet her! She seems so ... familiar.

Maddie pointed toward the woman. "What do you think she is selling?"

The driver looked surprised. "Her? I do not think she is a vendor here. I do not know her, but …"

The rest of his words were lost. Maddie Clare had already reached the woman. "Hi! I'm Maddie Clare!" she announced, as if that should have some meaning.

The woman beamed more brightly, and Maddie tried not to stare at the gold edges of her teeth.

I wonder how that works? Is that like a filling?

The driver started to say, "Uh, miss …" but the older woman had already extended a wrinkled hand, which held a small, wax-string necklace.

Maddie gazed at the treasure extended in front of her. It was obviously hand-carved, from a dark substance that held hints of green, black, red, and gold. Maddie couldn't fathom what the material was or if the color was natural or dyed. The old woman held the pendant in her palm and took hold of Maddie's right finger to trace the image. Maddie felt a shiver down her spine.

Then the woman offered the necklace to Maddie for closer examination. Maddie lifted it gently, almost reverently. The stone had a deep green hue. It was a circle, split down the center into one dark half with light images of gold and green and one light half with dark images of red and black. In the center, light and dark swirled together in an intricate carving, similar to a Chinese yin and yang symbol. Just out from this center spiral, four pyramids were carved, each with a tiny door, and out from there, four pairs of butterfly antennae at right angles to each other, like directions on a compass.

A waxed string ran through the top of the pendant and had a knot on each side. Without a word, the older woman showed Maddie Clare how the cinching mechanism worked to shorten and lengthen the treasure.

Maddie was absolutely smitten with the pendant, though it really wasn't her style. She glanced back to the driver, who was leaning against a palm tree, a hand on one hip. He tilted his head to one side and lowered his sunglasses to let Maddie see he was still watching. Then Maddie returned her attention to the old woman.

"How much do you want for this?" Maddie asked.

Hearing the start of negotiations, the driver stepped forward. But the elder woman raised her hand to stop him. She looked up at Maddie Clare and placed two fingers on the palm of Maddie's hand.

Immediately, Maddie saw in her mind the image of a large, white pyramid. Under the stairs was a barred door, slightly ajar. The vision, like those she'd received in childhood, was as clear as if she had been in it.

"El Castillo," the woman said, her voice sounding timeless and surreal.

Reeling around, Maddie looked to the driver to see if he had heard the woman's words. She gave him a questioning look, hoping he could translate.

His face was full of shock—and fear.

Maddie spun back around to see the woman was gone. Maddie searched left and right, looking down the hallways and scanning each window and doorway. The woman had vanished.

What the hell?

Maddie Clare could still feel the heat in her hand where the woman's two fingers had touched her, but all that remained was the necklace.

The driver shook his head in disbelief. He rushed to Maddie Clare with his hands outstretched in a protective gesture.

Bewildered, Maddie examined the necklace again. She looked up and down the atrium for the old woman. She was gone. Only the look on the driver's face—and the necklace in her hand—validated the woman had been there.

The driver's voice was tense and drawn. "I have *never*, in all my years driving around Cancun, seen anything like this. What did she say to you?"

"I'm not sure. Maybe 'El Castillo'?"

"Oh, yes. That means *the castle*. El Castillo is at Chichén Itza, a sacred place, not far from your hotel."

Maddie turned her focus to the driver. "I thought Chichén Itza was a pyramid."

"Chichén Itza is a sacred place. The pyramid called El Castillo is one of many structures there." His face remained thoughtful, but he continued to glance around, searching for the woman.

"Señor, what happened to the woman?"

"You did not see? She disappeared, right there in front of you."

Holding the necklace up, Maddie said, more to herself than the driver, "But, how will I pay for this? Where did she go?"

Unable to spot her in the market, the driver answered, "Maybe she sells some things at Chichén Itza?"

He made a motion toward Maddie, reaching for the treasure, but Maddie closed her hand and pulled away.

"Yes. Maybe I could find her there," Maddie said thoughtfully.

Maybe. But where did she go? How did she disappear?

Maddie turned back toward the parked taxi. "Let's get to the hotel," she said quickly. She didn't want her driver raising any more questions, nor did she want to be arrested for shoplifting on her first day in Cancun.

When they arrived back at the van, the driver slid the door open for her. Maddie climbed in, keeping the pendant tight in her hand, as though she had just found a lost artifact. She wanted to get to the hotel and get some privacy to examine her treasure more closely. Plus, she needed a shower.

And a drink.

With the driver focused on the highway, she began to subtly work the two knots on the string of the necklace, to see if she could get it open enough to wear. She didn't want to put it in her purse. When it was long enough, she tucked it down into her bra, where it would be safe until she could get to a mirror and cinch it up evenly.

What an amazing gift! Like a magical treasure has come from a pyramid and found its way to me.

What happened? Did that woman project that image into my head?

Maddie thought about all that had already happened on this trip: the full moon with its silvery reflections, the magical spotlight on the shoreline, another vivid nightmare, the happenchance meeting with the old woman who had given her the magnificent necklace, and the image that came into her mind when the woman touched her palm. She couldn't shake the feeling that the necklace had come from somewhere inside that pyramid, inside El Castillo. Maddie had the sense that her experiences had been preordained, and her heart and mind filled with anticipation—and apprehension—for what was to come.

When they pulled up in front of the hotel, the driver escorted her inside to the front desk. A young man greeted her and slid a registration paper in front of her. After reviewing it, Maddie gave him her credit card. Then she noticed people hanging out at the bar by the pool.

Now that's what I'm talking about!

Just then, Lynda walked up in a Caribbean-blue beach cover up, her blonde hair still damp from the water. "Hey Chickee-poo! We were expecting you hours ago!"

"Hey girl!" Maddie Clare wrapped her friend in a hug. "We stopped at Market 28 to get a few things." She fingered the little rope around her neck absentmindedly.

"Well, I'm glad you finally made it. Your room isn't quite ready, but there is a wonderful woman, Angela, who will take care of everything." Lynda walked Maddie to one of three ebony desks, where a dark-haired young woman stood waiting for them.

"Angela, this is my good friend, Maddie Clare. You'll take good care of her, yes?"

"Claro. Miss Maddie Clare, we are your family while you stay with us. I will make sure your room is okay and you have good success with your tours. How was your travel?"

"Good." Maddie thought a moment about showing her the necklace. Maybe she would recognize the image. Then, remembering she couldn't explain how she got it, Maddie opted to stay silent.

"I'll leave you in Angela's capable hands," Lynda said. "I have to take care of some things for the wedding. Be sure you find Kenz sometime. She's excited to catch up and hang out with you."

"I will. I'm looking forward to catching up with her too."

Maddie Clare turned back to the girl, who was peering into her computer. "Angela?"

"Yes, señora?" the girl looked up and exclaimed, "Oh. Your eyes are so beautiful!"

"Thank you." Maddie beamed, used to the compliment. "Do you know of a place called El Castillo?"

"Oh yes. It is a most sacred pyramid, a place of special significance for our Maya history. Are you going there?"

"Well. I am signed up to go on a tour somewhere on Sunday, some ruins by the ocean. But I would like to go to El Castillo instead."

"Oh," Angela said, looking at Maddie's itinerary, "You are scheduled to go to Tulum. You should be able to make the change quite easily because the same company handles both tours. Their office is just back there." She pointed. "They can make arrangements for you to go to Chichén Itza, where you will find El Castillo.

"Miss Maddie Clare, we have a room ready now. It is a bit separate from the others in the wedding, but it is no problem. This property is easy to find your way around. You are in the Blue Wing, at the end of the hall for privacy."

Angela swiftly went through all of the amenities then said again, "You must remember we are your family away from home. If you need anything, you must call me at extension 444. Don't forget my name is Angela," She grinned.

Maddie smiled. "Okay, thank you so much, Angela. I'll go to the tour company's office after I drop my bags."

"Yes, good. I will tell them you are coming. Sometimes for me to explain these things in Spanish can make it easier for you. Alejandro will take your bags."

"Okay. Thank you." Maddie turned and saw the expectant face of Alejandro, a very short man with jet-black hair, a crisp white shirt, and a brass name tag— "Guest Services."

"Onward," Maddie called to Alejandro, with her hand extending an invisible sword.

Alejandro led Maddie Clare to the far end of the property, pointing out the various restaurants, ATMs, and shops along the way. As they passed the Blue Wing's pool, he nodded to the cabanas where she could enjoy a drink. "The gym is back there, if you would like to work out."

Thanks for that, Alejandro. Getting to the room should be enough workout for me.

When they arrived at Maddie Clare's room, Alejandro put the key in the electronic lock and led the way. The room was crisp white, with orange curtains and chairs and a beautiful black-marble shower with glass doors.

Magnificent!

Maddie quickly tipped him and sent him on his way. She wanted to examine her necklace in private and get settled in.

Once the door closed, Maddie hurried to the bathroom and looked at her necklace in the mirror. She carefully worked the knots on each side of the pendant until it was exactly even and just the right length. Then she closed her hand around the pendant, trying to bring back the heat she had felt when the woman touched her palm. She recalled her words, "El Castillo."

Will it take me back to that place? Is the necklace magic?

She glanced at her watch, surprised at the time, and headed back down to the lobby, where she changed her Sunday outing from Tulum to Chichén Itza. Then she headed to the outdoor bar, just to see what they had to drink. Almost everyone had a margarita or daiquiri. "I'll take a mojito, please," she said to the bartender. He blended the green slushy swirl and, in no time, placed the drink in her hand. Maddie tipped him and smiled in appreciation.

Now that's service.

"Can I take this to my room please?"

"Yes, miss. Just let me put it into a plastic cup so you don't have to bring the glass back."

That takes a little class out of the experience, but what the heck. I get to take it with me. I love this place!

Maddie grabbed her drink and ran upstairs to get ready to meet the wedding party. She found the little wedding booklet and opened it to the itinerary and map. The bachelorette party was up on the roof deck, and she was already late. She slipped into a little black dress and dashed on a smidge of blush and lip gloss.

Arriving at the roof-top bar, she spotted the bride-to-be immediately. Jessica glowed like an angel as she glided from one cluster of guests to the next. She was a beauty, with huge blue eyes and shoulder-length blonde hair that framed her smile perfectly.

Jessica's eyes twinkled when she saw Maddie. "Oh my God, Maddie Clare, we were so excited when we heard you were coming. Thank you!"

Lynda's oldest daughter, Dani, ran up to join them. Dani's hair was a bit darker, but she had the same broad cheekbones and brilliant smile as her two sisters. All three of Lynda's daughters had spent years at the orthodontist, and they had million-dollar smiles to show for it.

Maddie Clare recalled a teenaged Kenz saying she wanted to be an orthodontist because they didn't do any work. They just told a dental assistant what to do, while they collected all the money.

She's a smart girl, that Kenz.

As if on cue, Kenz came sailing up in a blue dress. "Hi there! You made it! I thought you'd never get here."

"Ya, I got a bit delayed on the way here. Shopping, you know."

"I get that! Is that where you got the cool necklace?" Dani and Jessica both gave an appreciative nod as they saw the pendant.

"Actually, yes. It's kind of a crazy story. I'll tell you sometime when there's less going on. By the way, something came up, and I've changed my Sunday tour from Tulum to Chichén Itza. There's a pyramid I want to see …"

Dani piped in. "Oh … I know that one. El Castillo! Did you know that pyramid is the second-most-popular site for visitors to Mexico? More than one million people visit every year. It's considered one of the New Seven Wonders of the World."

Seeing the expression on Maddie Clare's face, Kenz rolled her eyes and said, "She Googles everything."

"I guess she does!" Maddie chuckled. "You know, it was pretty easy to change my tour. Would any of you like to come with? I'm a little worried the whole weekend will come and go, and I won't get to spend time with you …"

Excitement danced across Kenz's face, "Hey that's a great idea. I'll make an announcement later tonight and see if any else would like to go, too."

"Cool," Maddie said, as a peaceful happiness came over her. After a bit of small talk about the wedding, the girls were whisked away by other guests, and Maddie was left alone at the bar. She watched them mingle, feeling blessed they were in her life, yet wistful that she didn't have a family of her own.

As she ordered a margarita, she noticed the bartender watched her necklace the whole time. Maddie thought to ask him about it, but something in his demeanor felt a little creepy. She recalled how the driver seemed to want to reach for the necklace, to take it.

Maybe it's made of something valuable.

Maddie heard her Grandma Cora's voice, "Hold the necklace close to your heart, like a great secret. Not everyone will understand your gift." The voice seemed so close that Maddie gave an anxious look behind her.

Really, Grandma? Here? At a rooftop bachelorette party in Cancun?

Maddie's mind went back to the old woman in the atrium, and she replayed the entire scene, realizing only now that the woman had a similarity to her grandmother. Not in looks, and not just that they were both older. Something …

Perhaps she was wearing Grandma's perfume.

The details of her encounter were still so clear in her mind—and so weighty. Again she had a sense the encounter had been preordained.

Like a Jedi, the mysterious grandmother-crone moved the force of the Universe to give the farm girl the one necklace that would let her ... rule the world!

Maddie's face sobered mid-chuckle.

Maybe I've seen her in one of my visions. Maybe she's connected to those screaming children.

"Hey. Could I get another margarita, please?" As quickly as the bartender could make them, Maddie Clare knocked back two more margaritas and stood up to leave.

Maddie ordered a margarita in a plastic cup and headed back to her room. She was exhausted from the wild events in the market, a too-short night on the plane, and too many drinks with too little food. She wrestled the door open, kicked her sandals off, and flopped onto the bed.

That's enough for now.

Maddie thought she should learn a bit about the people she would be sharing her weekend with, so she pulled out the little wedding booklet. She began to flip through the pages, looking for her own name first to see what other people would know about her. But the alcohol and the long day soon took over.

Within minutes her breathing slowed and changed to a light snore, as the booklet slid to the bed.

* * *

The barred door of the pyramid was ajar, and nobody was guarding it. An uncertain push was enough to swing it open. Shivering as she sank into the cool air, she placed her hand on the cold wall to guide her footsteps while her eyes adjusted. Several feet down the hallway, she felt the edge of a door. Again, just a touch opened it. She entered a long, rectangular room. Two of the walls slanted inward as they rose. There were no windows, but she could see a slightly built individual with shoulder-length black hair hovering over a stone table.

Unable to make out details, she noted the individual seemed to be a young woman, maybe even a teenager, wearing an ankle-length tunic with a rope belt at the waist. The girl picked up a scroll from the table and wrote something at the lower edge of it.

Then it started—the children's screams. So close, perhaps just outside the walls. She ran back down the hallway, and as she neared the barred door, she smelled smoke. It was familiar, but not from candles or oil. She could give it no name.

She burst through the doorway. When she noticed the screams had stopped, she spun back around, but the pyramid temple was gone. She was standing on the edge of a clearing. Smoky haze surrounded her, blanketing her in its heavy, organic aroma.

The screams were replaced with the sound of bamboo poles "shap shap shapping" on stones. She recognized the distinctive sound from a childhood game. Combined with the smoke, the rhythm was intoxicating, and she began to sway.

Then she heard soft chanting. She peered into the clearing but could see nothing through the smoke. Turning toward the nearby jungle, she was certain she saw the grayish hue of mud-covered figures camouflaged against the trees.

No. It can't be them. They can't be here.

CHAPTER 3

The next morning, her head was pounding even before she opened her eyes, and the thick-headedness made her nauseous. Her heart raced—da-tum, da-tum, da-tum.

"Aaaagh." She couldn't make herself open her eyes but stretched out her arms to each side of the bed—as if self-crucifixion would be better than the throbbing—but after a whiff of stale-tequila sweat, she yanked her arms back under the sheets.

Did she also smell something charred and sooty? She sniffed the air, and the scenes from her dream drifted back. Though she had long-ago sworn off visioning, she gently tried to clarify the image, and it came into focus—a freshly harvested field, 40 or so Maya standing in rows of corn, and blue smoke drifting up from the ground. Somehow the smoke never rose above the Maya waists before dissipating.

Who were these people? And where were the tormented children who screamed for their lives?

Holding the vision in her mind, she tried to massage more detail from the scene without chasing the vision away. She slowed her breath, now more taken with the vision and the dream than the pounding in her head.

She watched the scene unfold. Forty or so men wore brown cloths around their waists and small black pendants around their necks. She reached for her own pendant and wondered at its similarity to theirs. The men reached over the cornstalks, left then right, working intently to pick up loose kernels that had fallen to the ground.

The women wore rust-colored tunics with rope belts. Their skin was dark and perfect, and their straight-cut hair was jet black. They, too, were gathering something, but the details of their movements were hazy.

The relentless pounding in her head soon reminded her of the chanting song of the night. An effort to remember its details was rewarded with a swift stabbing pain above her ear. "Ufff." She rubbed her eyes.

Still, the chanting pulse of the dream taunted her. In her dream-world, she heard the distant tribal echo of "Ya'ax muyal kan." Yet, strangely, the words had come to her in English "Blue-ue-ue-ue Sna-ay-ay-ayke Clou-ou-ou-oud,"

Hmmm. How is that possible?

The chanted tune was chopped up into a ceremonial pulse that matched the throbbing in her head.

Damn! I'll have this song stuck in my head all day.

She opened her eyes a sliver. The room was bright, telling her it must be near lunchtime. Her stomach churned at the thought of food, but a cup of coffee was definitely calling her name.

With a whole lot of cream.

She held the pillow tightly and forced her body into an upright position on the edge of the bed. Her feet touched the floor, but she knew she couldn't trust them to hold her weight just yet. Fluttering her eyelids as she adjusted to the light, she thought she smelled the essence of smoke. Maybe.

"Hmmmph." She shook her head to fend off the memories. It worked, but it also caused her to jolt upright with a new wave of pain.

Okay, Maddie! Time to get up!

She walked to the shower and turned on the tap, hoping a shower would ease the tension in her head and neck. As the water warmed, she choked down a couple Excedrin, wondering what all she had drunk the night before. She imagined the parasites that could be swarming through her body, having snuck in on an ice cube, drunk with tequila.

What was I thinking?

I was thinking I'd met a disappearing woman in the market who gave me a teleporting necklace. I was thinking it would be good to pass out and sleep without any screaming children or terrifying mud people. That's pretty much what I was thinking.

Steam rose up around her, and she closed her eyes, again seeing the smoke rising from the fields. She leaned into the stream of water then jumped back and turned the heat down. When the perfect, soothing temperature caressed her hand, she stepped under, tilting her head back to let the water wash away the disgusting smell of stale tequila and last night's perfume.

Wuff—that's some ugly stench, Maddie Clare!

She closed her eyes and let the water caress her for a minute or two. It soothed the tension in her neck and quieted her thudding pulse. But then a chaotic scene of people running, killing, and screaming came into her mind. Her eyes flew open to stop the images.

Was that a vision or a dream memory?

She had to know. Cautiously, she closed her eyes again and tried to focus on this newly recovered scene. Something about it seemed important, as if she was supposed to remember … *something*. She swayed her head back and forth, the water splashing against the back of her neck—left then right, over and over—as though the water would help clarify the memory.

The scenes began like a slideshow, much as they had in her first years of channeling the visions. First men with metal hats. Not British knights, but conquistadors. One wore a grotesque expression and somehow pulled himself close, as if he were in Maddie's face. She opened her eyes.

Did I just feel his breath on my face? Or was it the steam from the shower? What was I doing there? Did I fit into that murderous scene?

Once again, the line between dream and vision blurred.

If only I'd been above the dream, I could have seen what was happening. Strange it was from such an internal perspective, like I was actually there. I know I felt his breath! What is that?! Does that mean it was real? Does that mean the mud people are real? And the children?

She closed her eyes. What was the dream calling to her to remember?

Cautiously, she eased herself back into the zone (ready to spring out with a flick of her hair at any moment). Once she reestablished the channel, she saw from the corner of her eye a young man with dark shoulder-length hair. He wore a white-belted tunic and was running with paper scrolls in his hands. Maddie tried to concentrate, how many scrolls were there?

She should have known better. As soon as she focused on the scrolls, the scene faded, and she was back in the shower—a considerably cooler shower. She turned the tap back up to the once-frightening, full-hot level and poured shampoo in her hands. She finished her shower quickly, before the water could get cold, but she remained distracted.

Strange how real a dream can seem. Strange how some things come in night dreams and others come in visions.

Once out of the shower, she tugged on her denim skort and knit top. Thankfully, the headache had backed off. She finished her look with a pair of sandals and some lip-gloss, grabbed her key, and hurried out the door, hoping she could still get a late breakfast.

And maybe a bloody Mary.

She was slightly chagrinned to see breakfast had been replaced by lunch, but happy a few members of the wedding party were still nursing their coffee. She could tell they were with her party because of the "Sterban" sunglasses they wore. Jessica had included them in little gift-bags given to each guest. The glasses

were white with teal printing down the side—
"Sterban"—a combination of their last names, Stern
and Urban. Maddie Clare thought they were perfect.

Lynda stood up from the table, and Maddie called
out to her. She made her way to the table, setting her
hand on the back of the chair next to Lynda's mom,
Mary, who was finishing a plate of crêpes.

The waiter walked past with a pot of coffee. "Oh
please! Could I get a cup?"

"Yes, señora."

"And some cream too, please."

The waiter grabbed a cup from the next table, set it
on the table in front of Maddie, and hurried off. Maddie
thought she might grab some food before settling in.
"Will you guys be here for a bit?"

"I'll be here for about five more minutes, but then
I have to get ready for a swim with dolphins," Lynda
said. "Mom would love to have you keep her
company."

Maddie Clare smiled at Lynda's mom. "Perfect! I
need to get something to eat, but let's visit a while first.
It looks like I already missed breakfast, so I guess
there's no rush."

"Well it *is* eleven-thirty," Lynda said, smiling. "By
the way, where did you go last night, Maddie Clare?
Pretty mysterious, to leave without saying goodbye."

"Oh, gosh! I'm sorry!" Maddie blushed, realizing
she had been rude. Looking to change the subject, she
remembered the shap-shap-shapping in her dream.
"Hey, Lynda, before you go, do you remember what
they called that thing we used to do in elementary
school with the bamboo sticks—clicking them on the
sidewalk and jumping in between them?"

"I have no idea what you're talking about. Remember, I didn't come until the end of fourth grade. Maybe that memory is from before? You come up with the weirdest things, Maddie Clare! What made you think of that?"

"Oh … nothing. It was something from my dream last night."

"Huh. I wonder if that had anything to do with tequila." Lynda gave Maddie a little wink.

"Oh, I'm sure it did … and the long flight and those snacks they had out on the bar."

Lynda picked up her pocketbook. "Kenny and I are off to swim with the dolphins," she said. "Don't forget the rehearsal dinner at six, okay? We're in the Mediterranean restaurant by the Honeymoon Pools. Have you met the groom yet?"

"No. I haven't met him, or Dani's husband, either. I'll be there tonight, don't you worry. Have fun with the dolphins!"

The waiter returned with cream—*warm* cream.

You don't get that kind of service in America!

Gratefully, Maddie poured the hot liquid into her coffee.

Lynda's mom looked up from her cell phone. "Tinikling," she said.

"Excuse me?" Maddie asked.

"The bamboo dance. It is Filipino Tinikling."

"Tinikling. Yeah, that kind of rings a bell. From the Philippines."

Maddie Clare enjoyed reminiscing with Mary, though her stomach growled to remind her she needed to put some food in it. "What does Jessica's fiancé do?"

"He works for a company called Bending Branches. They make Kayak paddles. In fact, the whole wedding theme is built around the Bending Branches theme—because that's kind of how marriage is, bending in a storm, swaying apart and back together again, blossoming in spring and going quiet in winter."

"I love that idea! Leave it to Jessica. I'll look forward to seeing you tonight—and meeting your soon-to-be grandson-in-law. Right now, though, I've got to get some food in this belly. Then I'm going to try to find Kenz. I need some goddaughter time."

"Oh shoot. I think she went with Kenny and Lynda. But you will have time with her on Sunday."

"Sunday?" Maddie asked.

"Oh, yes. I think you were already gone when Kenz announced you were going to Chichén Itza on Sunday in place of Tulum. She asked if anyone else was interested, and there were a few takers."

Maddie grinned. "Oh yeah?"

"Yeah. Last I heard Kenz and Dani were going to try to join you, and Lynda too. I think she forgot to tell you just now. She's been running ragged ever since we got here.

"Ya, weddings can be a lot of work." Maddie felt a twinge of guilt she hadn't offered to help her friend more.

"Oh. It's not that. She's been taking on every adventure imaginable, from dolphins and parasailing to ancient ruins and fire dancing."

Maddie laughed and pointed a finger at Mary. "She gets that from you. You were always a fun mom."

"I was? Funny how we remember things, huh?"

"It sure is ..." Maddie said, more to herself than to Mary as her mind swished back into her recent visions and dreams.

Maddie told Mary goodbye and found the buffet, looking to settle her stomach so she could take a nice, solid nap. Once it was filled with breads and cheeses, she took her plate with her to the pool. Soon enough, she was stretched out on a cabana bed, feeling like royalty and hoping nobody would notice her.

Sometime later, Maddie was startled awake by the sound of shrieking children close by. She jumped up, nearly toppling herself, only to realize she had been wakened by children playing in the pool. When she jerked awake, she had the sense of coming out of a nightmare in full swing. It took a minute to get re-oriented. Relieved, she looked at the children, wondering how their little lives had led them to the Grand Oasis Tulum.

Then she remembered the wedding itinerary. She rolled over and glanced at her watch.

Four o'clock? I slept four hours?

Maddie sat up on the side of the bed, happy she wasn't in a beach chair, burned to a crisp. She watched the splashing kids and their families for a minute, wondering at the disparity between these kids growing up in luxury and the kids from her nightmares running for their lives.

These kids are real, Maddie. That's the main difference.

Maddie sighed. Though the doubt-filled, self-berating voice in Maddie's head sometimes backed off, it always returned. Maddie rose and walked past the families toward the beach, thinking a nice walk might clear her head. She watched the families, interacting on vacation.

No kids or family vacations for me. No kids graduating high school or getting married in Cancun, surrounded by friends. Just years of insurance claims. I need something more in my life than a job, a dog, and booze!

She glanced at the bartender as she passed but resisted the familiar urge. What she needed was a dose of fresh air, not a cocktail. When she got to the beach, she slid off her sandals to feel the hot sand under her feet.

The pulsing ocean called her name. *Maddie* as each wave came in, and *Clare* as it went back out. She stopped a moment to listen. *Maddie ... Clare ... Maddie ...Clare ...*

She longed to stay at the beach, soothed by the waves. She imagined spending the whole evening with the gulls and the gentle breeze, but a glance at her cellphone reminded her to hustle. Now.

Just in time, she forced herself back to the room where she quickly changed before heading to the rehearsal dinner.

When she arrived, she found her nametag at a table full of young couples, which made her wish she had studied her copy of the wedding booklet instead of falling asleep.

She waved to her goddaughter across the room. Kenz's blonde hair was striking against her blue dress. She was a beautiful girl.

I wonder where life will take her. Hopefully she won't follow her godmother's example of work, work, and more work.

Maddie sighed and settled in for an evening of food and drinks, along with pre-wedding games and trivia. Though she continued to be distracted by her recent experiences, she did meet a few people at her table, and by the end of the night, she felt like she knew Jessica and Andrew, as a couple, quite a bit better. The story of their meeting, dating, and engagement came to life through the jokes and speeches from friends, siblings, and parents.

She glanced over to Lynda, who was signing a conversation with Jessica from across the room. When Jessica had lost most of her hearing from a childhood illness, Lynda had risen to the occasion, becoming a strong advocate for the hearing impaired.

She's so happy and content in her life as a wife and a mom.

Maddie's mind drifted backward once again. When they were kids, people would have guessed Maddie Clare would grow up to have six children, while Lynda would become some wild radio personality, living the "high life."

Maddie recalled their "drinking years." Once when she and Lynda were high school seniors, they woke up in the hatchback of Lynda's AMC Pacer, having passed out at the end of a long trail of beers and bourbon. Yet here Lynda was, enjoying the fruits of her devotion to family.

Maybe there's hope for me after all.

Wistfully, Maddie raised her glass in Lynda's direction, silently toasting her friend's success. And, for the first time in a long time, she let herself feel hopeful for the future.

Later, having said her goodnights, she hustled along to her corner of the Blue Wing. When her room lights came on automatically, she giggled. "Abracadabra," she said aloud, waving an imaginary wand. She changed into a t-shirt and sport-shorts for bed. Then, peering into the mirror, she shook a finger at her reflection. "No more bad dreams, Maddie Clare!"

Sliding between the cool sheets, she realized how strange it felt to go to bed sober. She wondered whether she would ever fall asleep and decided reading might help. Reaching into the nightstand, she found a Gideon Bible.

Those Gideons were prolific—that's for sure.

Absently, she flipped through the pages, landing in Hebrews. "You are a priest forever, in the order of Melchizedek."

Who? Melchizedek? The "order of Melchizedek?" I don't remember that from Catechism, and what does it mean to be a priest forever? Wouldn't it just be during your career years? Or until death? What an odd way to say that.

The clock showed 11:33. She closed the Bible, clicked off the light, and let the darkness embrace her. The room was quiet—too quiet. Closing her eyes, she let out a deep exhale and drifted off.

She awoke with goose bumps running up her arms and her necklace strangely hot against her skin. As she reached up to touch it, the realization set in.

Oh my God, there's someone in the room.

She felt hot breath on her face. Her heart began to race, and she held her breath. The deep-chested sound of forced breathing was unmistakable, and she felt heat on the crown of her head. But how could that be? Her head was too close to the headboard for anyone to fit between.

Oh my God I'm going to die in Cancun! Alone in my bed! And sober!

Get a grip Maddie Clare!

She slowed her breathing, so she could hear his.

His? Its?

She sensed the apparition was male. It made its way down one side of her body, past her feet and back up the other side, like a full inspection. Yet the bed hadn't moved under its weight, not one bit. She trembled.

This breath is not human.

The breath was right next to her ear now.

Oh, my God! Oh, my God! I'm going to die of a heart attack.

The sound of the breathing grew faint, and the apparition seemed to move away, as if satisfied with its inspection. With her heart exploding in her chest, she barely raised her eyelids. She glanced to the right, moving only her eyes. There it was a—*something*— next to the window.

What the hell?

As though it heard her question, it approached her, this time from above. Without thinking she raised the covers to her chin, covering her necklace.

Oh God! I just moved! It saw me! I know it saw me move.

The apparition drew closer, and now she could see it, a grayish dragon's head, like an ancient Maya glyph, translucent, like a balloon. It breathed through a jagged nose, its mouth twisted in a macabre sneer.

An apparition—or maybe an entity—from another dimension.

The form continued its inspection, entirely too close to her face, back and forth, left to right, down the length of her body. It hovered for a moment at her feet and then … vanished.

Gone! It's gone!

She didn't move, for fear she was wrong. The seconds felt like hours. Then, just as she was about to reach for the light, the bed began to shake.

CHAPTER 4

Instantly, Maddie sat up. She saw the TV rattling across the bureau and her suitcase shuffling on the desk.

"Waa ..." she cried out when she heard her shampoo fall with an ominous THUD into the bathtub.

An earthquake? Really, God? Right now? Here?

The shaking stopped as suddenly as it had begun. Silence. The hot breath was gone, too. 3:33 AM.

Jesus. What was that? An apparition?

Just then, her phone rang. She grabbed it, nearly knocking the Bible to the floor.

"Maddie Clare?"

"Ya," she whispered. Then she coughed nervously and tried again, "Ya?"

"Did you feel that?" Lynda asked.

"An earthquake, right? What do we do? Will there be tremors? Do we get up and go outside, like a fire drill?"

"I have no idea. You're the disaster adjuster. Is your cell phone there? Maybe keep it with you in case anything weird happens."

"Ya, I have it. And Lynda?"

Say something, Maddie. Anything.

"Yeah?" Lynda asked.

"Oh, nothing. Just, uh—take care of yourself, huh?"

"I will. You too. Good night."

"Good night."

I should call her if anything weird *happens? Weird?! Where would I start? She has no idea!*

That's right, Maddie Clare. She has no idea. No idea at all, because you never tell her—or anybody— anything! So now you can either explain the visions, the messages, the channeling, and everything else that's happened over the past thirty plus years—or you can let her enjoy this weekend with her family while you stay quiet.

Maddie lay in bed with the receiver in her hand, not sure what to do or think.

I'll just get through the next couple of days. When we get back, I'll tell her a bit and see how she responds. I have to talk with somebody about all this. Someone who knows I'm not bat-shit crazy.

She chuckled at the metaphor. The *thing* had looked a little bit like a bat. She wondered what she might have done to bring on an experience like that.

I had dinner, and I didn't eat anything weird. Only one glass of wine. No aspirin. Nothing.

That wasn't some weird dream, Maddie Clare! Not even a vision. You were awake, dummy! Awake!

She hung up the phone but left the light on. Then she lay back down and closed her eyes, forcing herself to bring back the memory. The breath, the grotesque image. The apparition was frightening, but it didn't actually seem menacing. Just more … curious.

I'll never be able to explain that to anyone.

Glancing back at the clock, she was surprised—4:44 AM.

That's weird. Wasn't it just 3:33?

Maddie remembered something Ruth had said. Angels use triple digits when they're trying to get your attention.

That bat-thing was no angel!

She lay there in the dark a few minutes more, wondering about the bizarre beast-thing and how the experience could have been possible. Was she losing her mind? Getting early dementia?

She was sure she'd never get back to sleep, but the next thing she knew, the light was glaring and bright, even with the curtains closed.

Immediately, the memory of the apparition came back to her.

Was that a dream? Did I imagine it?

The earthquake had been real, and the call from Lynda had been real as well. She knew that much for sure.

Throwing back the sheet and duvet, she twisted to the edge of the bed and put her feet on the cold floor. The room seemed so normal in the daylight. She got up and opened the curtains, squeezing her eyes shut as the sun invaded the room. "Ugh," she said aloud, "I need a walk to shake off the night!"

After a quick shower, she slipped into a dress and clipped back her still-wet hair. Stealing a quick look in the mirror, she noticed the pendant was greener than the day before, when more gold had come through.

Just before leaving, she walked to the window and took a half-hearted peek behind the curtain.

Only after letting the curtain go did she realize she'd been holding her breath. Wanting to clear her anxiety, she half hoped she would see Lynda and half hoped nobody would be around. She peeked out of the stairway. No Sterban sunglasses at the Honeymoon Pool this morning. She hurried past the main dining room and toward the cabana bar.

"What'll I pour you, miss?" asked the bartender as he gestured to the "morning alcohol" —Baileys, Jameson's, Tia Maria, and champagne for mimosas.

"Uh, none of that. Just a coffee with cream, please."

"Sure." He turned his back and used a cappuccino burner to heat up the cream for her coffee. "Did you feel the earthquake this morning, miss?"

"Ya! Scared the Bejeezes out of me. Does that happen often?"

"No. Maybe three or four times a year, but it's always scary. We believe an earthquake is a sign something extraordinary is coming."

Ha! In my case, it had already been there.

She tried to sound light. "Not this time, I hope. My friend's wedding is today, and we wouldn't want anything *weird* on its way to that."

"No. That is for certain. You are with the big wedding party, eh? This is a beautiful place to get married. We see big weddings here all the time. It is quite beautiful to see all the bright colors and different things people do with their ceremonies." His English was perfect, though his accent was strong.

She accepted the coffee, with fresh hot cream, and slowly the ocean waves drowned the sound of the bartender and his customers. But they didn't drown her feeling about the night before. She played it all back in her mind, the hot breath on her face, the racing of her heart. It had seemed ominous, there in her room, sizing her up. In hindsight, it seemed that if the apparition *had* seen something it didn't like, things could have gotten ugly—like something out of a 2AM horror movie.

And just what, Maddie Clare, do you imagine the bodiless beast was going to do to you? Suck on your neck like Dracula? Beat you about like a scene out of Ghostbusters? What exactly do you mean it could have gotten ugly?

"Hmmph." She set her cup down with a resounding "CLINK" and left a dollar on the bar.

Just then, Lynda walked up, chuckling. "There you are, at your favorite hangout, I see."

"Actually, I'm heading out for a walk on the beach. Care to join me?"

This could be a chance to talk with her, at least open the subject.

"Can't. Today we're parasailing, but we'll be back by one for the wedding."

"It's not until four, though, right? They didn't have any trouble from that tremor last night, did they?"

"No. Jessica said her perfume fell and the bottle shattered. But nobody got hurt. Andrew cleaned it up."

"What? Isn't the groom supposed to stay away from the bride the night before the wedding? Maybe that's what brought on the tremor."

Dropping to an ominous, masculine voice, Maddie said, "The gods have been angered."

Lynda laughed and gave Maddie a quick hug. "Well, Chickee-poo, time for my parasailing! Oh—hey! We got our tour changed. Kenz and Dani and Reed and I are coming with you to Chichén Itza!"

"Oh my God! That is so cool! I was really worried I wouldn't get any time with you because of your busy adventure schedule. Speaking of which, good luck! Or maybe break a leg? What's the right one to say?"

"I think *good luck* is plenty. Thanks."

"Okay. Well, good luck. Use plenty of sunblock!"

Lynda went on her way, and Maddie headed to the beach, floppy hat in hand. The resort owned a pristine stretch of shoreline, where the waves made a perfect morning dance. The beach was deserted, and she was glad. She slid off her sandals, so she could feel the cool morning sand. After walking awhile, she looked back at her path and remembered the "Footsteps" prayer her grandma had mounted on her wall. "One night I dreamed a dream …" It was all she could remember. She repeated the line over and over in her mind.

She plopped down on a bit of dune at the end of the resort building. Sweeping the hat from her head, she allowed the breeze to blow her dark hair back from her face. She hung her head a bit as she sighed and covered her face with her hands. She wondered what she'd been thinking coming to Cancun, where she seemed fated to spend more time having surreal experiences than catching up with dear friends.

Another heavy sigh, and she turned her mind to the dream she'd had her first night in Cancun. She replayed each scene of the Mayas doing their Blue Snake Cloud Dance, along with the Tinikling sound. The chant had a reverent quality, and she wondered how the words had come to her in English, rather than the language of the native Maya people.

Maddie sensed the chant was an expression of gratitude—for everything, from the breath in their lungs to the harvest and the community. She allowed the sacredness, reverence, and pulse of the chant to fill her with the perfect rhythm of the world. Just as Mayan words had come to her in English, she knew the feeling of the people, even without being told. There was one beat, one pulse, one single, swelling tide.

The scene with the screaming children returned to her. She closed her eyes gently and nudged herself back into the zone. Soon she saw metal-capped conquistadors throwing every horror imaginable at the simple tribespeople.

Were the conquistadors the ones killing children? It didn't seem to be the people in tunics—and certainly not the reverent people in the fields.

But no, that didn't seem right. The scene with the screaming children seemed separate from the one with the conquistadors. She said the word aloud, "con—key—sta—doors."

Why do you visit my dreams?

She allowed herself a few more minutes of viewing, replaying the dream in full and then backing up to replay it, a single frame at a time. Afraid to "vision" more information than she was ready to know, she shook her head lightly each time she started to slip too far into the zone.

I may have gotten away with visioning last night ... but then there was the apparition and the earthquake. Maybe better to leave the visions alone for now.

Something about all this seems important. Like there's something I'm supposed to do or remember. Maybe just one more peek. I want to know who that man was, running with the scrolls.

Maddie again called up the vision, pausing at the young man carrying the scrolls, gently trying to massage details from the scene. Suddenly, a new realization jolted her back to the beach.

It was a woman. The same woman from the room behind the door! A young woman with an armful of scrolls with those marks she made at the bottom.

She closed her eyes again, trying to follow what happened to the young woman, but it was useless. She couldn't get the image back, could not close out the sound of the soothing waves or the caressing Cancun sunshine.

She glanced at her cell phone. Three o'clock! She bounced up and jogged down the beach. Less than 50 feet later, she was completely out of breath, huffing and puffing as loudly as the apparition.

I've got to start working out.

She came around a curve and saw the wedding chairs, all lined up on the beach. *Shit!* She broke into a full run, and by the time she reached her room, the sweat was pouring down her face. After a quick shower, she pulled her hair back in a braid and slipped into her sun dress. She brushed on nude eye-shadow and a touch of lip-gloss. When she was ready, she had fifteen minutes to get into her seat.

The wedding was a blur of pink dresses, white bows, and khaki pants. Maddie's seat was between two young families with preschool age children. Though she knew there were a few single people in the group, most of the guests were already married with kids or living with a significant other.

It's so unreal how different people's lives are. Even Lynda's and mine. From similar childhoods to adult lives that couldn't be more different.

The bride and groom said their vows. The crowd chuckled as Jessica promised she would never drive in the left lane unless she was passing another car and that she would never put leashes on their children. Andrew promised to never keep score, even though he usually wins. He promised to be with her through good times and bad times, through Packers wins and Vikings losses. Light and laughter were clearly an important part of the love this couple shared.

The reception was held at the rooftop bar, under the magic of the stars. Jessica's father, Kenny, stole the night by signing Heartland's song "I Loved Her First" to his hearing-impaired daughter.

> I loved her first
> I held her first
> And a place in my heart will always be hers
> From the first breath she breathed …

Maddie felt the sting of tears as couples held onto each other, and even strangers put their arms around the people next to them. Kenny and his daughter locked eyes and his hands formed the words. Maddie had always thought signing was elegant and beautiful, but now she knew more of its depth and poetry.

Maddie Clare felt a hand clasp hers. She didn't recognize the lady, except that she was one of the wedding guests, but she felt a moment of unity with the crowd, witnessing the blessed moment—as sacred as a father receiving his newborn daughter for the first time.

Everyone's eyes brimmed with tears, awash in the love of a father for his daughter, giving her to her groom, but reminding him that first she had been his. Maddie felt a hand slide through her arm from the other side. It was Kenz, with tears streaming down her cheeks. Maddie pulled her closer and tilted her head to touch her goddaughter's.

No entities or mysteries here. Just love.

Nobody wanted the song to end, but of course it did. A momentary hush was followed by a raucous outpouring of clapping, cheering, hugging, crying, and well-wishing. Maddie wished love would always be that way, that every person could feel that kind of devotion from a father—or from anyone.

Reluctantly, she allowed Kenz to slip from her grasp. The young woman ran off to embrace her father and sisters. Maddie ordered another Malbec as she watched the family from the bar. She now felt removed from the wedding party, separate and distant, as if she were seeing them in a vision.

The last tears in her eyes were for herself, how alone she sometimes felt, how she longed for connection and meaning. Her life seemed so empty compared to Lynda's. If she wasn't intended to be married and have family, why had God created her? It couldn't have been for visions and nightmares.

One for the road. I'm too tired for monsters, demons, or screaming children. Not tonight.

She ordered her last drink in a plastic cup and picked up her handbag. The deck was full as Maddie glanced back to the couples dancing, the bride and groom tending to guests and loved ones, and Kenz talking excitedly to her sister.

Maybe one day ...

With that, she turned to climb the empty staircase. The floor-level sconces cast eerie shadows on the walls, and the night was silent but for an owl hooting in the distance, "Hoo, hoo."

Oh, who yourself, Mr. Owl. Not me. That's who.

The banter with the owl lifted her spirit a bit. She swung in a circle in the courtyard, dancing with the moon. She lifted her cup in a toast to herself.

Time for a change, Miss Maddie Clare. New job? New home? Something has to give.

She hoped tomorrow's adventure would move her closer to her "something new." She had always wondered at the ancient temples and pyramids—what had happened to the people. How could technology, incredible enough to create pyramids and gold sculptures, along with complex languages and mathematics, just vanish?

Ruefully, she thought back to her college days. She'd managed to take only one class in her major—a class on hieroglyphics—even though digging for ancient treasure had been her dream.

When she reached her room, she changed into night clothes and brushed her teeth, noting the pink slurry in the sink when she spat out the last of the evening's wine.

That's probably the first thing that needs to go. It's certainly not done my skin any favors—or my hips.

She tried to settle into bed, but she was restless. She propped up her pillow, casting her hand behind her neck as she stared at the ceiling, thinking of who she had been as a girl. After the visions stopped, she'd had a lot of free time to invest in her hobbies. She was always setting up a card table in her bedroom, and spending hours on jigsaw puzzles, never stopping until the last piece was in place.

She had been a precocious child, often sitting in the hayloft for hours, sometimes even after she'd stopped visioning, just to stare across the fields and listen to the wind speaking her name. She remembered, for the first time in a long time the floor of the barn. It had something like linoleum flooring under the straw, and it looked like an old-world map.

I'd love to see that again. Maybe it was *a map. A real one. The barn was old.*

Her mind shifted from one errant topic to another. Moments from childhood—attending the church's adoption picnics with her brother, accidents on the farm, and conversations with her grandparents. Moments from high school—music and writing awards and a completely dateless senior year. Nothing, it seemed, would calm her mind.

Come on, Maddie. The journey to Chichén Itza starts early. Get to sleep!

Over and over, she flipped her pillow. She shifted and shuffled through an agitated night, seeking a perfect position, but her mind continued down its restless path. She finally settled on her back and closed her eyes gently.

Maybe I can bring up some nice, pleasant images to help me fall asleep.

Maddie slowed her breathing and held her eyes loosely shut. She relaxed her shoulders into the pillow, took another deep breath, and shifted a bit more. As she exhaled a deep breath, the first image appeared, and the familiar, soothing feeling returned to her.

How she had missed the unfolding of her mental slide shows! The visions from her early years had been especially simple and soothing. Grandma had been there to help her understand them—or at least to help her accept them. For so long, they had been a refuge.

When they had become more complex and detailed, she often wished for her grandma to coach her. But Cora was gone by then—and long gone by the time the nightmares had come.

This image stream—the scientific equipment— was her favorite. She looked down from above on copper equipment. Carefully, she navigated the room, while holding herself in *the zone*, ever so careful not to engage her conscious mind. No people. No conversations. No interaction. Just a silent slide show. First, a ledge, about a foot deep, held brass equipment that she now knew was a sextant and a surveyor's level. To the right of that, she could see a small window above a stove, and then …

Wait! What was that? Did I fall asleep? Did my alarm go off?

Maddie Clare strained to listen, thinking the apparition might be back, but the only sound was the breeze through the palms. She opened her eyes and looked at the clock.

5:55 a.m. Again, with the triple digits—weird! Angels? And the necklace is warm! Does it gather my body heat while I'm sleeping and somehow radiate it out again?

She looked about the room before reaching for the light. Once she was sure there were no more entities, she slid her arms under the covers to linger in the warmth of the bed. She tried to return to her vision, but it was useless.

Something woke me up. A woman's voice.

In her mind, she heard it again, "It all changes today, Maddie Clare."

The voice was familiar. The woman from the market? Grandma? Are you here?

She could not recall any dreams from the night, just the images from before she had fallen asleep, and there weren't any women in those. She shivered when she heard it again— this time aloud.

"It all changes today, Maddie Clare ..."

PART II:

THE INITIATE

CHAPTER 5

Unable to shake the feeling that she had heard the message out loud— "It all changes today" —Maddie couldn't get back to sleep. Not that she had time to sleep anyway.

Vowing to ask Ruth about the triple numbers, she got out of bed and dressed for her big day. All the while her mind wrestled with this latest surreal moment.

She dabbed a bit of sunblock on her nose and took a final glance in the mirror, cinching the knots on her pendant to the just-right length. Then she looked at her watch: six minutes to get to the lobby.

She hustled across the property and found Dani and her husband, Reed, sitting on the front step. Lynda was propped up against the nearby valet podium. Maddie shivered at the chilly dawn breeze. "Isn't it six-thirty?"

"Yeah," Dani said. "The bus should be here any minute. Where's Kenz?" All of this, Dani said with an air of authority and control. She was the eldest sister, after all.

Lynda sat up, "She's sick, maybe a touch of the brown-bottle flu. Six-thirty is pretty early the morning after a wedding."

"That's too bad," Maddie said. "I really wanted to hang out with her today. I think Chichén Itza is going to be amazing. Do you know if there's any coffee?"

Lynda, pointed toward the door. "On the main lobby bar. But you better hurry."

"Cool. Anybody else?"

Dani piped up. "Yeah. Sounds perfect. Two sugars, please."

Maddie Clare hurried across the quiet lobby and poured two cups. Then she glanced at the bottle of Irish Cream behind the bar.

It all changes today, remember?

Glancing at her reflection in the bar-back mirror, she shook her head.

Pfft. Sure, it does.

Maddie hurried back outside to join the waiting game. Nobody was talking, which was fine with her. Maybe because of the voice that morning, or maybe because she had been praying for it, Maddie really was expecting something major to happen today. Something would change. She was poised for great adventure—or great catastrophe.

The arrival of the bus interrupted her thoughts.

"Good morning," Dani said, approaching the driver with the group's receipts. He took the papers from her hand and glanced through them.

"One minute, please. I must check you out of the hotel for the day." Before they could say a word, the 40-something driver ducked inside, the receipts in hand.

Check us out for the day? Like library books?

"Really?" Dani scoffed, apparently thinking the same thing. "Then again, at least he's almost on time. I've heard nightmare stories about groups waiting hours for guides who never showed up."

"You know," Maddie said, nodding toward the door, "he probably just needed to pee and wanted an excuse."

"Ewww," Lynda said. "He can keep my paperwork!"

The man reappeared. "My name is Manuelo, and I will drive you today. We must go now so we will be on time."

Maddie tossed her empty cup into the trash. "So, Dani, do you know if we tip him when we get there or when we get back? And do you know if Chichén Itza has an ATM?"

"The website said no tips because drivers are paid for their service by the tour company, but it's probably not a bad idea to stay on his good side, just in case."

"In case what?" Maddie asked. "Don't even talk about things going wrong. It's been a weird weekend."

Dani shot Maddie a querying look and pulled out her cell phone.

"Sorry, I didn't mean to sound cranky. I need some sugar."

"Oh yeah? Is that it?" Dani lifted her eyebrow at Maddie Clare, giving her the opportunity to say more, but Maddie let the moment pass.

Their group was the last to get on the bus, and the only open seats were in the back two rows. Reed, Lynda, and Dani settled in the very back, which was two steps up from the rest of the bus and offered a great view.

Maddie opted for the single seat in front of them, which was better suited for sleeping. As she got settled, reality sank in. Today she would visit one of the world's greatest archaeological sites —El Castillo at Chichén Itza. She smiled to herself.

Maybe this pyramid will inspire me. It all changes today.

Despite her excitement, Maddie was exhausted and fell asleep before the bus reached the highway. Her slumber was deep and dreamless.

Sometime later, the bus left the paved highway for a gravel road. Karung.

Maddie sat up and looked around the bus. She noticed a man a few rows up who was looking her way—staring, in fact. When she adjusted her pendant, his interest seemed to increase.

Maddie glanced down, thinking he might be staring at her ample bustline.

When the man stood up, Maddie said a silent prayer he wasn't headed her way.

Her prayer was answered. The man went to the front of the bus and picked up a microphone. "Good morning, ladies and gentlemen. My name is Renato, and I will be going with you on your trip to Chichén Itza. I am a Maya priest and happy to answer questions. Can everyone hear me?"

An appreciative murmur could be heard throughout the bus.

"First, I will give you your snack box, so you can eat whenever you want. Be sure to drink plenty of water, or you can get dehydrated. The jungle is very humid and hot."

As the priest spoke, Maddie found something about his presence uncomfortably familiar, but she knew she hadn't seen him before. The man's jet-black hair framed a round face that matched his well-fed paunch. He was quite a bit taller than Maddie, which surprised her. Most Maya she'd met—in fact everyone except her original taxi driver—had been her height or shorter.

Does he remind me of someone? No ...

Apprehension once again replaced some of her excitement about the ruins. The priest continued his spiel for the tourists, but his voice faded from Maddie's awareness.

Is he *part of everything changing today? Hope not. He's ... not creepy exactly ...*

Jeesh, Maddie Clare. Enough of the mystery and intrigue. Today you will enjoy yourself. And your friends. And your interest in archeology. That's change enough.

The priest was staring at her again. *Oh nuts. Did he just ask me something?* Maddie waited for an indication of what, if anything, she was expected to say, but he continued his narrative about the tour and the restoration of the site.

Meanwhile, Maddie's insurance-adjuster mind counted 65 passengers and multiplied that by the $75 trip fee. The tour company's gross sales would be nearly five grand. She glanced up, pursing her lips.

I wonder how much of that goes to our driver, Manuelo—or to the restoration?

Humph. Probably not much.

The priest walked back up the aisle, giving people bottles of water and white pastry boxes with fruit, cheese, and crackers inside. Handing one to Maddie Clare, he said, "Where did you get your necklace? Did you purchase it here?"

Purchase?

"Uh, yes. In the market when I first arrived." Her face grew hot, as she felt herself put on the spot. She hadn't actually paid for it and couldn't say where she had gotten it. She didn't even understand it herself. The pendant grew warmer.

"It is very nice, a spiritual symbol of sorts."

Dani jumped in, "Of sorts?" She reached for her phone, ready to Google at a moment's notice.

"It is the symbol used for Hunab Ku," the tour-guide said. "It is called the Galactic Butterfly."

"Galactic Butterfly," Dani muttered as her thumbs flew across the tiny keyboard. "Let's see … The symbol was created as a representation of the One God concept when colonists came to the Maya world and wanted to convert the Maya people to Christianity."

"Yes. Hunab Ku means One God," the priest said. "The symbol was not originally Maya, though we have used it for so long many of us do feel it as part of ourselves. I think the name was first used around the 1600s. But the idea of spiritual Oneness cannot be credited solely to Christians. Hunab Ku was a way of combining the Christian idea of one God together with the Maya cosmology."

"The Galactic Butterfly shows us that many truths fit together into one whole—including things that might seem to be opposite, like heaven and hell, light and dark, above and below. They are all part of the

Oneness—completion."

The priest continued to gaze keenly at Maddie's pendant as he spoke. "First, because it was such a big idea, Oneness had no symbol—just the concept was enough—like having no image for God. Then, because it was difficult for the foreigners to explain and discuss this idea, people began to use an image similar to the one on your pendant.

"The Galactic Butterfly image has been transformed many times in the past forty years or so, by people from different countries, to become the popular symbol it is now. You will often see it in the markets, used by Toltec and Zapata weavers as a New Age symbol."

A few other passengers turned to see what the priest was talking about, stretching their necks to see Maddie's necklace.

Great. I don't really need a bunch of people asking about my necklace. It's not like I can tell them how to get one for themselves.

"You seem to know a lot about it." Maddie said. She was distracted, trying to reconcile the image she had seen when the woman gave her the necklace with everything the man was saying.

"Thank you," the priest said. "I am a Maya priest, first, but I also have a bachelor's degree in theology and archaeology. My education is of great assistance in my work as a priest of the Maya cosmology."

So, it's like your personal—Christian, Maya, archeological—symbol, eh? Get your own necklace, Mr. Priest Dude!

Maddie's stomach churned, and she felt lightheaded. She took a swig of her water. Noticing the pendent felt quite cold, she stretched her legs out on the seat, thinking of a way to change the subject. "Are we nearly there—to El Castillo?"

The priest replied. "Yes, we are nearly to Chichén Itza. El Castillo is one of the pyramids at this very important ceremonial site in Maya cosmology."

Maddie rubbed her chin with her thumb, shielding the necklace from his gaze. "What kind of ceremonies did they hold there?"

The priest cleared his throat. "Well, the name Chichén Itza translates to "at the mouth of the well of the Itza people." This well, or cenote, was the site of many human sacrifices as part of religious and agricultural ceremonies."

Dani piped in, "Is cenote with an *s* or a *c*?

Ignoring her, Maddie sputtered, "Did they sacrifice children?" Her mouth went dry and her head began to spin. She felt a rolling wave of nausea welling up from her gut.

The priest eyed her with half-closed eyes, a little too intently for her comfort. Maddie averted her eyes. "Sometimes," he said.

The word hung in the air, heavy with implication, and the priest's pensive expression led Maddie to believe there was more to be said about this sensitive subject.

"Ah!" Dani said, relieving the tension, "It says here a cenote is a kind of giant sinkhole where the layers of limestone have given way. There's usually water at the bottom. The one at Chichén Itza is 130 feet deep."

She turned to Reed with her phone to point out some detail. "Man, I hope no limestone gives way today." Just then, she exclaimed, "Look! We're here!"

The priest turned, "Yes, we are. Don't forget, you must be back on the bus at twelve-fifteen because the bus will not wait for you. If you miss this bus, you must pay $135 US for a taxi back to your hotel. Now you have about ten minutes before meeting your guide to the ruins."

"You aren't our tour guide?" Dani asked.

"No. I'm not a tour guide. I'm a Maya priest who does ceremonies. One of the local Mayans will be leading your tour as I take care of other things."

Other things? What other things does one do at Chichén Itza? And why *does this guy feel so familiar?*

Practicality took over the moment as everybody gathered their bags. Maddie looked back to Dani, "Hey, what did you find out about those ATMs?"

Dani laughed. "Yeah. They're in the food court, where modern commerce meets ancient culture. Gotta love it."

When the tour group stepped inside the courtyard, Maddie's head swam.

Is this motion sickness? That's never been a problem before. Why do I feel so weird?

"Sorry, Lynda. I've got to get another bottle of water or something. I'm not feeling right."

"Oh, no! I hope you're not getting sick."

"Huh? No, I'm sure I'll be fine. I probably shouldn't have had coffee and cream on an empty stomach."

"Yeah. That would do it for me," Lynda said. Then she jumped a little. "Hey! Look at that! I'd swear your necklace was green, but now it's nearly black." Lynda lifted the pendant from Maddie's chest to peer at the details.

"Really?" Maddie took it back and tried to see, but the string was too short. She definitely knew is was cold, though. Ice cold. "Huh," she said, trying to sound calm. "I think I'll find a ladies' room now and splash my face.

Lynda touched Maddie's arm. "Hey, don't get lost, okay? Do you need a Dramamine? Want me to hang with you?"

"No on the Dramamine and the escort. You go ahead. I'm probably just a little dehydrated. I'll catch up."

Maddie waved Lynda off and found the door that read "Mujeres." She ducked inside and splashed her face with cold water. It felt refreshing, but she continued to sense that something was just … wrong. Her knuckles turned white as she fought another wave of nausea.

How did I go from the excitement of an archaeological adventure to grabbing a sink in a public bathroom? I hope it's not some parasite!

She took deep, soothing breaths and lifted her necklace closer to the mirror.

Well, Lynda's right. It really looks black now. I can barely make out the green and red, though I see a bit of the gold. Now I know why it doesn't look more Maya. It's not Maya. It's probably a mood necklace you can buy at any gas station down here. So much for my sacred artifact, whispering to me from the ancient world!

What do you think is going to happen, Maddie Clare? Is your Galactic Butterfly going to turn Butterfly Galactica and sweep you into space? Get a grip, girl.

With that she dried her hands and turned for the door. Maddie's need to experience El Castillo overcame her upset stomach. She stepped out of the bathroom into glaring daylight, just in time to see her group huddled around the new guide. Maddie hurried to catch up.

Lynda was some distance away, but Maddie was right next to Dani, who whispered, "See that thing he's holding up?"

The man held a long sheet of parchment in the air for all to see. It was covered with teal water-color images. He said it was a report of an individual's Maya Nahuals, something like an astrological chart. Maddie noticed the top image was very similar to the apparition she had seen in her hotel room.

"Sounds like something right up your alley," Dani said, flashing her a sideways grin.

"You're right. That *is* my style—and what a great keepsake!"

"You're supposed to pay the lady over there. Then you pick it up before we leave."

Maddie jerked her head up, hoping to see the older woman from the market, but it was a Maya woman about Maddie's age, in a long gray skirt and white blouse.

The tour guide started walking up the steps. "Here we go," Dani said, grabbing Reed's hand.

"Hey," Maddie said, "I'm going to buy one of those charts and hit the ATM. I'll catch up."

"No problem. We'll watch for you," Dani said.

Maddie hurried over to purchase her Maya Nahuals. She wrote her name and birthdate on a little form and handed over her credit card.

The transaction was quick, but by the time she looked up, her group was at the top of the white stone stairway. She thought she'd better catch up with them, rather than getting cash and a bottle of water. She hustled for the stairs and noticed the priest standing a few feet away, watching intently. With a shiver, she picked up her pace to join the others.

About 40 people stood between her and Lynda, and she couldn't maneuver between them. And, though she tried, she couldn't spot Dani and Reed at all. Maddie figured she'd catch up with them later.

She trailed behind the group, which was leaving the wide courtyard by way of a bridge so narrow only two people could walk abreast—and that was only if nobody was passing from the other direction. She wondered if there was another exit. Looking ahead, she saw only the shoulders of strangers. In her peripheral vision, the jungle seemed to close in around her.

She pondered the jungle as the crowd inched along.

I wonder what the jungle's like when it's raining. If you stand under a tree, do you get wet, or do the huge leaves keep the rain off you, like an umbrella?

Maddie Clare couldn't see the guide, but the jungle seemed to be acting as a megaphone.

She listened closely to his explanation of the white stones on the path. "These stones pick up the moonlight, even the smallest bit of light, and reflect it into the darkness. This let people on pilgrimage to Chichén Itza travel at night, as well as in the day."

White stones lighting the trail naturally? What an intriguing idea. Maybe my new place will have a courtyard, and I can try this out.

The path opened to a manicured lawn, and Maddie

got her first glimpse of Chichén Itza. Immediately, she knew it had *something* to do with the mud people nightmare. And the children.

Is this where I was chased?

She wiped the sweat from her forehead. No question she was anxious. A nebulous tension surrounded her, and for a moment she wished Lynda knew about the nightmares—and all the rest. She glanced around behind her, feeling a bit of relief when she didn't see the Maya priest.

If anything happens to me today, nobody will know about the weird things that came before.

At that moment, the mighty El Castillo came into full view, transforming Maddie's fear into awe.

Magnificent! That *is what I saw when the old woman touched my hand.*

Her eyes caressed the pyramid. A temple graced its apex, and each elevation had its own massive staircase. Her chest swelled with the desire to run to the pyramid, climb to the top, and see all the world below.

Though she heard his voice, the guide's words were lost on Maddie. She was entranced. Using her binoculars to get an up-close view, Maddie wondered about the people who had stood, ceremoniously, at the top.

What power they must have held, the evangelists of the Maya. They must have lived like gods!

The group had completely circled the pyramid. The other tourists were taking photos with their phones and iPads, but Maddie could not take her eyes off the towering structure.

This is all too familiar. It feels like ... coming home. This must be the pyramid in my nightmares ... where the children screamed.

Maddie looked around for a sign of something terrifying, but she saw only beauty. She reached for her pendant and ran her fingers over it, as if reading Braille. She tried to lengthen the little rope to see the image, but it was hopeless. Like a boy tying his first Windsor knot, she was lost without a mirror.

She vaguely noticed a warm vibration from her necklace as she turned her binoculars to the top of the staircase, focusing on the shadowed openings where gods once reigned.

No wonder you always see Maya priests depicted wearing huge headdresses. They must have looked tiny, standing way up there.

Maddie scanned the face of the temple walls, trying to see if any of the stones had carvings or inscriptions. She thought she saw one that looked a bit like the Galactic Butterfly.

Can that be? I thought the image wasn't Maya. I wonder if the temple at the top is newer than the rest.

She peered intently through the binocular lenses to find the image again. At the same time, she touched her necklace, willing her hands to compare the two. Trying to establish a starting point for a thorough scan, she followed the staircase down to the bottom, where she noticed a barred doorway.

There!

It was the doorway from her vision—as well as her nightmares! Her heart beat faster and her stomach roiled. A movement in her peripheral vision caught her attention. As she turned toward it, her head swam, and her world went dark.

CHAPTER 6

Suddenly, inexplicably, Maddie found herself in a stone chamber. She looked around, trying to figure out where she was and what had happened.

Did I faint? Is this a clinic? Where's the door?

Maddie silenced her mental chatter to listen. Nothing. Quickly looking about, she saw no light source—no candle, fixture, or window—yet the room was filled throughout with soft light. She was still clutching her necklace, but the binoculars were gone.

Did I drop them? Was I mugged? Where am I? What kind of mugger doesn't take a necklace?

She tossed her dark hair back, closed her eyes, and took a few deep breaths. As her breath calmed, she noticed the necklace matched her body temperature and then warmed just a bit. She opened her eyes again and looked around the room, looking up to a ceiling so high she could give it no measure. Nor could she guess the square footage of the room. If she started walking, it would take a few minutes to reach the other side.

Like the room in her dream, this one had a stone table. But this table was much larger, long enough to accommodate at least six people on each side, and the room was much bigger.

Is this room sealed, too? How did I get in here? And, how will I get out? This is no clinic.

Checking the space again, she found nothing but the table and the inexplicable glow. Softly, she whispered, "Oh my God, how did I get here?" She bit the inside of her cheek, working the flesh back and forth between her teeth. Then she looked around, yet again, confirming she was alone.

Right then, she heard a voice. "Do not be afraid, child. You are safe. Safe inside the great pyramid of El Castillo."

I know that voice! It's the woman's voice from this morning! "It all changes today." Inside the pyramid? How is that possible? Did I pass out?

Maddie turned around, full circle, finding no one. The hair rose on the back of her neck, and goose bumps peppered her arms. "Who's there?"

"My name matters not. Think of me as a Keeper of the Universe."

Maddie Clare tilted her head to one side, trying to visualize the woman. The voice was mysterious and slow, with the fullness of maturity, not the girlish pitch of youth. It soothed Maddie and inspired her trust. She wanted to know more.

"Are we … inside the pyramid? How did I get in here? Who are you?" The words tumbled out of her mouth in a panicked frenzy as she pivoted forward and back peering through the glow for the source of the voice.

"More importantly, Maddie Clare Owens, who are *you*? Why are *you* here? And what is happening in *your* life."

"Wait! You know my name? How do you know my name? And I don't know why I'm here! I certainly didn't plan this!"

Shut up, Maddie Clare. You are in a ... a pyramid, with a ... a someone ... who is trying to tell you something. Shut up.

With a chuckle, the voice said, "You are wise, young one. This would, indeed, be a good time to listen. This space will give us privacy from the world for a few minutes. You are safe. Your friends have not noticed your disappearance, and we have some time for you to learn about the workings of the Universe.

"You've been having some *experiences* that show your former life no longer fits you. You are entering a new stage. If you choose, you can take a different road from the one you've been walking. I will help you to understand this shift in your life.

"What you have been experiencing—what you might call a mid-life crisis—is what we call the *Illumination Station*. You have reached a crossroads, and the Illumination Station is the Divine's way of shedding light on your life, on the way you respond to and interact with events and people. This is a time when you will re-evaluate your life as it is now and how you would like to live in the future. From this time forward, you can choose to fly, walk, or sail through your life. What you decide at each step will determine what comes next.

"I know you are confused and a little frightened, but I assure you this will make your life better. There are universal truths that govern this planet. These are things we all know on some level. We all know and understand gravity, with or without a book to teach us. When we drop something, it falls.

"Yet there are many ancient laws, forgotten truths, that today's scientists have yet to discover and name. The law of gravity existed forever before finally being *discovered*. In fact, natural laws have always existed on this planet. They are only named when discovered by man."

Makes sense. Germs existed before we knew of them. They were only named upon being discovered. The Oneness of the Universe existed before the Galactic Butterfly.

She smiled, touching her pendant, surprised at the calm that had settled over her.

The voice continued, "Some things a scientist might call superstitious and other people might dismiss as New Age, like fate and chance, also run according to universal laws. *Everything* runs on universal laws. There are *reasons and rules* for everything, whether humans understand and name them or not.

"Even things that don't have a definable *reason* still have a *cause*. One example that's still unproven on your planet is that thoughts actually manifest. The thought or necessity is the cause, but the magnetic pull of the thought or need actually creates its reality. While many people believe this about prayers, they haven't correlated it to their daily thoughts. Thoughts just aren't measurable—*yet*.

"One day the pull of thoughts and needs will be acknowledged as fact, just as gravity has been. It will be understood that the timing of manifestation is determined by the energy, emotion, and intention behind the thought, multiplied by universal need. If someone invents something they need for themselves, the pull can be weak, but if there is a worldwide need, a thought can manifest with miraculous speed. No other outcome is possible.

"A thought that is in alignment with someone's original life purpose will also manifest at great speed. The speed of outcome is also affected if high emotion is driving a thought or prayer. You can see why this law of "manifestation by thought" is difficult to prove. Many variables are involved.

This is a bit cerebral for me, but I want to understand. Is this why I am here? For this ... voice to teach me about this law?

Maddie Clare leaned back against the table. She set her hands on the cool stone, relaxed her shoulders a bit, and shook her head, hoping to clear some of the thickness. The contrast between this experience and her "real" life—of insurance claims, evenings with Maybelle, and too much wine —hit her hard. Her heart sunk a bit at how lost she had felt for years.

This place feels more like home than home does. This is what I've been seeking—spiritual learning, knowing, and experiencing—like an archaeological dig into universal truths.

The voice interrupted her thoughts. "Now, let me share with you a bit of your own history. Remember the dreams that wake you in the night? The ones with the screaming children?"

Maddie nodded her head, dumbfounded by the thought of her bedroom, her most intimate space, being observed.

Does she see all of that? What is she, my personal angel? Is she behind the triple-numbers?

Responding to Maddie's concerns, the voice said, "It's not as though I am hovering at your bedside, Little One. But everything you think and do becomes a part of the universal consciousness—the matrix. We'll come back to that. Right now, I want to show you your past and your connection to this place, as shown in your dream."

"*Show* me?" Maddie's voice was weak, as she imagined sailing off like Ebenezer Scrooge with the Ghost of Christmas Past.

Then, toward the center of the space, a holographic image appeared, a scene from Maddie Clare's recurring dream. Now, though, there was no screaming. She heard only the woman's voice while the scene unfolded.

"You were there," the voice said, lighting up the holograph. "Truthfully, you were *here*, at Chichén Itza, in a room on the other side of El Castillo, near the barred door. Even from the other side of the pyramid, you heard the children screaming. They named this place Chichén Itza—*at the mouth of the well of the Itza people*—in reference to the cenote.

"People were sacrificed here, in the cenote, to create the scream. It is difficult to understand now, but the scream was thought to serve a higher purpose. It was a *cause*, like I mentioned before. It created a magnetic pull to bring the rain or sunshine for the crops.

"You were a scribe, a young woman, at that time. You worked in this temple, transcribing the codices, some of the most sacred ancient wisdom."

Oh my God! The girl in my dream! The one with the scrolls. That was me!

The hologram shifted to a different, smaller room. It, too, was lit by a sourceless luminescence. "That's the room I saw when I received my necklace!"

Maddie's words had slipped out, and she was suddenly afraid the necklace, which she hadn't paid for, would be taken from her. She enclosed it in her hand.

New Age or not, this necklace is mine now. I can feel its significance to me.

The holographic scene continued, and Maddie refocused on the narrow stone table, which now had a roll of parchment stretched across it. The young woman, the one with jet-black, shoulder-cut hair, was leaning over the parchment, intent on her work. Just then, Maddie heard faint screams; the scribe's head jerked to one side.

The girl covered her ears with her hands and moved her lips fervently, apparently in prayer. Then Maddie Clare heard the girl's thoughts as if they were her own. "I will come back! I will come back! I am sorry I am too small to save you. I will come back. I will protect other children, in your name. I will come back and keep this from happening again."

Tears streamed down the young woman's face, as the last scream—and the holographic image—faded from the room.

In spite of its heartrending events, this vision frightened Maddie far less than the nightmare. Maddie Clare was looking in from the outside, a distant and safe observer, as she had been in her childhood visions.

While she still felt sadness and tension, she knew nobody was being hurt in the present moment.

The woman's voice began again. "That was you. In another lifetime, you were here. You swore you would come back to help these children and all the children of the world. That promise is another intangible cause, with a thread of soul memory that still reaches you. Your intention was so fervent it still pulls at you, demanding the promise be kept. And because of its great strength, the pull of that promise reaches others as well."

Soul memory? Mine? And it reaches others?

"You are more than you think, Maddie Clare, more than you remember. In that life, you learned many universal truths as you recorded them. And *you* saved the codices; doing so was your final act in that life. You have seen this."

"The young woman who ran with scrolls clutched to her chest!" Maddie whispered under her breath.

"Yes. You hid some of the codices in secret places, and they remain hidden even to the present day. All of those secrets are woven into who you are, and you can access them within the matrix of universal consciousness, which surrounds all things and holds all memories."

"Huh?" Maddie tilted her head and frowned, trying to follow what the voice was saying.

This would be so much easier if I could see you.

Without responding to Maddie's thought, the voice went on. "Did you notice the numbers at the bottom of each scroll? They are codes that identify the scribe and the information contained within them, something like your library system of coding and filing."

Maddie had indeed noticed the markings and wondered about their significance.

The woman continued. "If the dream should come to you again, take notice of the people. You will recognize some of them in your current life. Three of you swore to return and protect the children—to bring comfort and protection to others in their name. Two of you are on the path. One of you is lost."

What? How will I recognize people from that time in my current life? I don't look anything like that young woman. She could almost be a boy. Am I one of the two? Am I the one who is lost? Why "two" are on the path but one is already lost? What a strange way to say that. What am I supposed to do?

"Though the scribe you were in that lifetime was a woman, gender does not have to be the same from one human lifetime to another. In fact, sometimes part of your life purpose is dependent on being born to a particular gender.

My child. I know you have many questions, but our time is limited. Another will come to you who will explain more about the promise. For now, you must understand more about the workings of the Universe; this is more important than learning about who you have been. More of that will be revealed with time."

The voice began to fade. "Remember one more thing, Maddie Clare: as you hold a thought in your mind, the matrix makes it accessible to others as well."

Maddie Clare jerked up to full attention. "Wait. Are you leaving? Please don't go. I don't understand."

The voice grew tired and faint. "Another Guardian of the Ancients—a priest of the Most High God—is coming to you now. Because he is of a higher order, he can hold earthly energy longer than I. He will teach you more about universal energies and the Illumination Station. You may recognize his name. He is Melchizedek."

"Wait! *Melchizedek?* The guy from the Bible?"

There was no answer. The woman was gone.

CHAPTER 7

From the silence, a man's voice—resonant, soothing, and mesmerizing—entered the space. "A key lies within you, Maddie Clare, nestled deep within your cells. It is woven from your ancestral memories and DNA, in confluence with your soul's experience and knowledge, gathered during many lifetimes. While these memories would seem to be erased during your physical birth, they can be accessed when activated in a particular order."

Activated—in a particular order? A personal conversation with someone from the Bible? About my inconsequential life? Really?

Maddie felt the very breath-of-life had come to share wisdom with her. Tears welled in her eyes from indescribable awe and deep reverence, and she again felt the pulse of her pendant vibrating softly, as though it had its own pulse.

"I will convey images directly into your mind, Maddie Clare, so you may understand my words better. This will etch pathways in your brain, so recalling the ideas will be like remembering a favorite movie. Close your eyes and experience the universal matrix."

Maddie Clare closed her eyes and found herself completely surrounded by an endless star-filled night sky. The darkness and the lights themselves had a liquid quality. Some light-points seemed brighter than others. Some got brighter then faded. Together, they created a kind of grid. In the distance were spans of darkness, where it appeared some lights had gone out like light bulbs. These voids created a magnetic pull; they sent a beckoning energy into the darkness, a universal whisper, "Relight this point."

The entire matrix of grids seemed to breathe. It expanded and contracted. Lighting went up, and lighting went down. New areas were lit. For a moment, Maddie was reminded of life in the ocean, suspended and floating. She wondered if she was seeing hydrogen or matter; perhaps the nature of the substance was one of those undiscovered truths the woman had eluded to.

I should have taken chemistry in school.

Melchizedek began speaking again. "You, like all human beings, are an ever-changing liquid light form, made up of energized matter. Your physical body acts as a vessel that enables you to impact your surroundings and enjoy the sensual experiences of being human. In deeper truth, your body is the liquid, and your soul energy is the light. You are the soul that animates and energizes your physical body, making you a liquid-light being.

"To this union with your soul, the body brings its own cellular memory. The body holds the unresolved traumas—along with the talents, gifts, physical training, and education—of its ancestry. The body remembers the time spent in the mother's womb, as well as the experiences of her lifetime and her mother's lifetime."

Maddie Clare marveled at the holographic scene. A child zoomed backward in time, all the way into its mother's womb. Then the child's mother traveled back through her own life and into *her* mother's womb. With the pace of a high-speed light rail, time kept rolling back. Among the many scenes, Maddie glimpsed clothing and hairstyles from her earliest childhood visions.

"The soul also has memory, but in order to have a human experience, previous lives are erased from conscious awareness. Instead, people are given clues— experiences like your early visions and dreams—to remind them of who they are and why they came to this human life."

The holograph had a hazy texture, and Maddie saw a number of scenes replayed from her recent visions and dreams. Once again, scene after scene came from darkness into view and then back to darkness. El Castillo—Greece—Egypt—and a place that did not seem to be of this world.

"Wait, are those *my* lives?" Maddie Clare's eyes flew open, causing the hologram to vanish.

Melchizedek continued. "The family you're born into, the community you grow up in, your birth location, gender, date and time: all of this sets you on a trajectory to have certain experiences. Your soul and body memory combine with the circumstances of your life to activate you toward the life you were born to live."

Maddie closed her eyes gently and was relieved when the hologram lit up again. She saw images of Beaver Lake, her parents, and her friends. The pace of the images slowed, and she was able to see details clearly. She reached her hand toward the images, even though they were in her mind.

"Many human beings experience this activation as a confluence of life lessons, natural talents, and single or recurring events—a calling that says, 'This is yours to do in this lifetime.' From within the matrix a particular point of light is beckoning, affecting you, magnetizing you to certain situations, dreams, and people.

"This is because human beings are the *breath and pulse* of the grid. You are its *life.* Every person—each liquid point that you are now seeing in your mind—is constantly changing from minute to minute, continually shifting the vibration and light of universal consciousness. Each day, each moment, of your physical life, you light up a different sector of the grid because you are ever-changing and because what you say and do interacts with others.

"What you hold in your memory banks is different at the end of each day than in the morning. It is different after lunch than it was before. Even one hour or one minute—even if you are sleeping and dreaming—can change everything. You know better than many that a single dream in the night can profoundly affect your life."

The holographic image shifted again to a gray-haired man taking a nap and dreaming. Maddie could actually see inside his dream. Then she saw him wake up, run to his desk, and scribble rapidly. The scene transitioned to his being on stage in front of an applauding audience. Then she saw conversations among distinguished people, perhaps professors or scientists. Then he was back on stage, a larger stage, receiving an award of some kind. Maddie leaned toward the hologram to try to make out the letters.

"Nobel! Oh my God, the Nobel Peace Prize ... From a dream?"

Melchizedek would not be deterred from his narrative. "Yes. Even from a dream. This is one way the grid is sometimes adjusted. There are light-workers—you would call them angels—who are tasked to help direct information to individuals. Many of these individuals will not act on the "pings" of information, but when one person does, it changes the dynamics of the grid, energizing various light points, and magnetizing even greater interest. Manifestation is the only possible outcome.

"As each human thinks, feels, interacts, and moves, he or she changes the grid. No two humans have ever held the same exact energies or information. You can see why. No two people have exactly the same DNA, cellular memory, soul memory, and experiences. For two people to have the same exact energies is one of the few truly impossible things in your world.

"Conscious thoughts, which you see here as liquefied light points, interact with the grid, so every moment has the potential to change everything for everyone.

"When a soul is not in human form, meaning the human body has died, its interactions with the grid have a subtler quality, like a soft breeze blowing through a forest—untouchable and unseen—as you are experiencing me right now."

The image in Maddie's mind revealed a man working in his garden. One minute, he mentally reviewed his "To Do" list. The next minute, his body was lifeless on the ground.

Maddie felt a drop in energy, similar to when an airplane engine is powered down. On the grid, a number of light points dimmed, like a brownout. This made sense to her, but she was surprised by what happened next.

The man's last breath hovered above him for a few moments, and Maddie sensed a momentary but distinctive shift in the energy, a tightening. Maddie saw a rapid review of all the things in his life that he had intended to say, all the tasks he had intended to do. Each image hovered for a just moment, until he let it go.

Maddie saw the bright light that so many speak of following near-death experiences. She saw the man choose to enter the light, letting go of everything he had not accomplished while in physical form. Then the final breath of his life wafted through the air and dissipated, taking with it the lingering tension.

Bloop! His physical energy was gone, like a floating bubble popping in the air. Only his essence remained.

Then, in the room within El Castillo, Maddie sensed a light, masculine breeze. She opened her eyes, knowing she had just felt the man from the garden— his *essence.*

Like Melchizedek, here, only more like a ghost.

"Huh," Maddie whispered, in awe. "That must be what happens to ghosts; they don't let go before their physical body dies. They get stuck in-between."

Melchizedek pressed on. "The physical, interactive human being now becomes an essence, a hydrogen entity. The soul continues to have an effect, but the transition from liquid energy back to pure essence—like the transition from water to vapor—completely shifts the being's impact on the grid. The things the person had *intended* to do or say, the things the person had intended to *complete*, are now pulled off the grid, like water becoming steam that dissipates in the air.

"Many of these unfinished things are inconsequential, like intending to get new tires on the car tomorrow, but when a person leaves the intention of their birth—their life purpose—unfulfilled, the loss ripples throughout the matrix."

Three light points got dimmer in one area of the grid.

How can that be? How can three people blow off their life purpose?

"To turn from a life purpose, Maddie Clare, is not so difficult. It begins with a small diversion, but change grows exponentially from its point of origin, as when a ship's captain adjusts the heading only a few degrees but ends up worlds away from where he would have been or could have been.

Or maybe should *have been.*

Maddie felt overwhelmed by the thought. An avalanche of decisions she'd made (for better? for worse?)—suddenly needed, all at once, to be reviewed.

"Not every decision hits on a life purpose, Maddie Clare. As humans, you have free will, so even decisions that impact your life purpose are yours to make. When one turns from a life purpose, someone else will have a purpose that's similar. That person's purpose will be activated when the first person strays.

"But no two beings are exactly the same, and each individual brings a life purpose to fruition in a different way." Melchizedek's voice took on a fatherly tone. "You see, Maddie Clare, turning away from a life purpose is not ideal. Life purpose continues to be of great importance, and its call should be heeded.

"All people come to this physical life in order to have a soul-human experience—a life of purpose—but some get sidetracked by worldly distractions, such as money, power, sex, food, drugs, and alcohol.

"Others—like you, Maddie Clare—use distractions to drown the call of a life purpose that frightens them. It is far better to heed the call." Melchizedek paused.

Why is he telling me this? Far better to heed the call? Or what?!

"Sometimes, in order to impact the grid rather quickly, a soul may drop in to help re-balance the matrix. This is often the spiritual, matrix-level cause of adoption. The child is born into one family, picking up its DNA, unresolved traumas, gifts, and talents. Yet, the education and experience they need in order to achieve their specific life purpose must take place elsewhere.

"This was the reason for *your* adoption, Maddie Clare. Your adoption moved you to your rightful place on the grid, so you could become a light carrier.

A light carrier? I came here to change the matrix? I'm an insurance adjuster who drinks too much.

116

"You are being asked to shift your trajectory, Maddie Clare, to remember the original call. You have turned away from the visions of your childhood due to your misunderstanding of their meaning. You were a child then, but you are not a child now. Now is the time for you to return to your original life purpose."

"But I don't remember who I am! We lose those memories when we are born."

In response to her thought, a liquid flame scrawled on the wall of the pyramid: *Illumination Station.*

Maddie jumped and screamed a little bit. Moses and the burning bush came to mind. Then she stood, dumbfounded, staring at the flaming letters.

Melchizedek's voice deepened. "*This* is what you were born to do, Maddie Clare Owens—to channel messages like this one and then to broadcast the messages, to help people understand the grids and the matrix and the universal truths. You are to help them change their way of thinking. And you will help them light up their part of the grid; part of your life purpose is to help others remember theirs."

Maddie's body tingled at the implications of what he was saying. She recalled the woman's voice telling her she was at the Illumination Station, the point in life when you re-evaluate, while you can still make dramatic changes.

Folding her hands together, she raised them in a closed prayer, and pressed them to her lips. She recalled the spotlight she'd seen from the plane and how it and the full moon revealed every detail of the shoreline. Now the spotlight was on her.

The holographic image showed her being received by her parents at the adoption agency. Then it sped rapidly through her baptism and earliest childhood experiences, moments she didn't actually remember.

But my cells do remember.

Shit! What was he saying? My adoption?

"When too many people have strayed from their life purpose, the grid loses some energy and can become unbalanced. Then souls come into life to adjust the grid for future generations. Often, these individuals will not birth children of their own because it would make such an irrevocable ripple in the matrix. They might try, but something stops them. Sometimes an accident takes away their ability to have a child. Others will lose a baby to miscarriage or still-birth."

Maddie sighed deeply. "Oh, no…"

Realizing the implications for her life, she whispered, "Is there no other way?"

Melchizedek's voice softened, "You were called to reactivate some of the darkened light-points in the matrix in this lifetime. As long as someone remembers the information, there is access to it. Regardless of your claims, you do remember much about the universal truths you've learned through your lifetimes. Your memories are being reawakened. This is the reason for your dreams and for your recent strange experiences. You have only to wake up and remember.

"Remember the image of the man who died and became essence? The same is true of any physical thing when it dies or is destroyed. The entity's potential to provide proof—be it a book or scroll or hieroglyph—is now erased and cannot be recovered."

Where is this going?

The hologram transitioned to a scene of documents and scrolls being burned. Image by image, over decades and centuries, documents and artwork were burned, smashed, pulverized, or destroyed in water. Maddie Clare felt salty tears stream down her face as she watched the slideshow of destruction and the ensuing dimming of liquefied light-points.

As Melchizedek continued, the hologram transitioned to a scene of dinosaurs. "The discovery of dinosaurs and creatures that no longer live on this planet demonstrates how the matrix is impacted by dimming and lighting of the grid. At one time, this planet held many dinosaurs, but all memory and evidence of them was lost until someone *discovered* a bone, then an entire dinosaur, then more dinosaurs, and so on.

"So long as a shred of artifact or evidence remains, the proof is accessible. As one person starts to investigate or read about ancient existence, the light and energy of the matrix begins to grow—until the energy itself draws the discovery of the proof.

"Like the missing books of the Bible? Like the bodies under Easter Island?" Maddie was thankful to grasp the idea, but it was difficult to gauge whether she got it right.

This would be so much easier to understand and believe if I could actually see this Biblical man.

Melchizedek responded, "Then the focus would be on what I look like instead of on the information.

"Yes. You humans have a dire need for evidence, validation, and proof.

"The very pendant you wear is made of greenstone, from the time of the dinosaurs. It carries not only the energy of a New Age symbol of One-source; it also carries the energy of the time when dinosaurs roamed this planet. Some people will only have to see and experience the Galactic Butterfly crafted in such ancient stone to begin their sacred activation. Even if you have no direct conversation or interaction with them, they will feel the pull of the energy of the grid, calling them to the life they were born to live."

Maddie jumped, clasping her hands, "My necklace! That's why everyone stares at it—not necessarily the symbol but the energy. It's the magnetic pull that people respond to. That's what happened to me when I saw it! I responded to its energetic pull! That's why the temperature goes up and down, and the colors change."

A hint of mirth came through Melchizedek's voice, "Yes, it has a pull. Many things have a pull. Like dragons, like visitors from other worlds, like Noah's Ark."

As the last words hovered in the air, Maddie could feel a tightening of the grid. She watched closely to see where it was lighting up and was rewarded with several points taking on a higher luster.

"Aha!" She pointed, though the image was in her mind.

No wonder I was brought into this sacred space by myself! Anyone else would think I had a mental disorder. But why me? I'm no Indiana Jones. No Livingston. No Einstein.

Then again—oh my God!—the possibilities! I have to start visioning again. I must pick up my messages!

Maddie Clare! Pay attention!

Melchizedek continued patiently, and Maddie sensed he had paused to allow for her digression and excitement. "This pyramid, known as El Castillo, is built on a vortex energy field—a place where the laws of the Universe are amplified. There are many of these locations on your planet, where people can become activated to shift and illuminate their section of the grid, thus achieving their life purpose.

"As certain areas of the grid are forgotten, they lose their energy. Important and integral information can be lost. Sometimes it is completely lost and requires a drop-in, like you. Other times, it lingers out of sight for a long time but returns to human consciousness when it is reactivated, perhaps through a story, a magazine article, or even a cartoon.

The hologram cleared for a moment, and her eyes opened to the space where she was standing. *Illumination Station* was still flaming on the wall, with the glittering texture of a handheld sparkler.

"The room we are in now—and the technology that built the pyramids—has been long forgotten by human beings, forgotten even by the Maya people. However, because these are sacred sites, infused by sacred teachings and built on an energy vortex, they still shine brightly in the matrix.

"Because so many people visit and interact with this structure called El Castillo, it is only a matter of time before this room is relit and the information hidden here is revealed. A few people have been given "pings" to seek and know more about this location and the people who lived here.

"Our presence and our conversation in *this space* today will help to force its rediscovery within the next five years."

On the grid, Maddie saw a very bright light-point, showing the energy of their conversation and their presence inside the pyramid. She sensed increased tension in the space around the light and imagined her Galactic Butterfly glowing, as she saw the image of scientists *discovering* the room within the temple of El Castillo, where she was standing now.

"Wow! Shouldn't present-day technology reveal these energetic truths?" she asked aloud.

"Perhaps one day, scientific truth and spiritual truth will be revealed to be one truth, but that has not happened yet."

For a moment, Melchizedek was quiet, and Maddie could feel the tension increasing in the room. For once her mind wasn't racing to and fro. Instead, she felt anxious that his voice had stopped.

Tensioning is right ... this is a moment of tightness.

Timidly, she spoke again. "Melchizedek?"

"Child, there is another side to technology, which I will speak about only briefly. Some of the technology that has been created in the past fifty years represents great advancement."

The grid displayed an area that was quite bright, reminding Maddie Clare of a gas refinery, with lights everywhere.

"The technology of magnetic resonance imagery and satellites has brought great healing and communications to your world. However, certain individuals and groups are using these technologies to seek out and control missing artifacts that are meant to be held until the correct universal time for their rediscovery. These gifts are being stolen. Some are being locked away, and others are being destroyed."

Again, his voice fell silent as Maddie Clare digested the meaning of his words.

Are they being literally destroyed, like the paintings in the holograph? Surely, he doesn't mean that.

Holographic images sped past so quickly that Maddie could only try to grasp details. She could not respond emotionally to the images' content. There was no mistaking the slamming and locking of doors, the images of lasers coming through the stratosphere and photographing things beneath ice caps, pyramids, mountains, and monasteries.

She whistled lightly, "Oh. That's bad."

"Maddie Clare, please do not think of things as bad or terrible. Especially, do not do so with any great emotion. You must always stay in the light and in the positive. Once you reactivate the universal truths of your memories, you will learn more about the importance of impacting the grid in a positive way.

"All humans must learn to respond to situations by empowering the positive and thus energizing each situation with light and love in order to improve its trajectory. While the body and environment are biologically affected by thoughts and emotions, the essence of the soul is light. Ancient people were *masters* at bending this light.

"But that is for another day, Maddie Clare. You will come to recall and reactivate these truths, if you choose, in a way that is balanced and loving.

"More importantly, as you move forward on this journey, you must remember that ink is liquid and thus resonates particularly strongly with human, or liquid-light, energy." Melchizedek paused again, allowing the impact of his words to settle into her body and add tension to the grid.

Maddie's stomach dropped as she recalled everything she touched with an ink pen—greeting cards, post-it notes, check blanks, credit card slips … She imagined the liquid of the words that flowed through her hands, hoping appreciation had been conveyed.

"This is where books and scripts and scrolls become so very important. One day, science will fully understand the vibrational properties of hydrogen and carbon and how each material has a harmonic resonance that is definable and traceable.

"From loving thoughts to logical thoughts to hateful thoughts—the intention, beauty, and truth (or lack thereof)—carried within words energetically combines with the writing itself to affect the matrix in a more powerful way.

"This is always true, whether the words come from one individual or from the conscious thought-input of many, like the Vedas of India. Once a thought, word, or idea is written—even if it is just written privately, like your automatic writing—it is in the universal consciousness and available to all, forever, even after the printed material is gone."

My journals? They're in the universal consciousness? So, if I burn my personal diary—Oh, this is way too much to take in.

"Universal consciousness holds all the memories of every thought and intention, but written thoughts and intentions add more energy to the matrix. People on this planet revel in proof. This is why objects of antiquity are given such great credence.

"The very word *artifact* relays that they are to be trusted as fact until proven to be false, as the root "fact" actually means "something that is made." When people believe there is *evidence* out there—like evidence of Noah's Ark or the missing books of the Bible—they will search and search, write and write. This energizes the grid immensely and allows that artifact to be discovered.

"Many ancient wisdoms are being held in undiscovered scrolls, paintings, hieroglyphs … and artifacts. Yet too many individuals have gotten distracted from their life purpose—to reveal these missing bits of information—and those artifacts are coming precariously close to losing their physical form."

Maddie wanted to be sure she understood. "So, the basic difference between a thought and an actual book is only that the print book, many years from now, provides evidence?"

"Maddie Clare, this will not be the last time we meet for you to receive messages. For now, I want to make sure you understand the power of thoughts and prayers. When thoughts or visions are charged with emotion, the way prayers are, they have incredible power. When prayers for healing come from a number of humans at the same time, even more energy is added to the energy quotient, increasing the magnetic pull for healing to manifest."

The holographic image transitioned to the scene of a child with a tumor. Frame by frame, Maddie watched as those who loved the child silently prayed. She could hear their thoughts and feel the intensity of their emotion. The tumor shrank, and Maddie nearly cheered out loud when a doctor showed magnetic images, confirming the tumor's disappearance.

"Recently, humans have become more aware of the energetic workings of the Universe—the matrix—through books and movies. These works offer diverse aspects of universal wisdom, and they are good. Through them, people are changing, trying, believing, and experimenting. Many people are activating—at least taking the first steps in activating— toward their life purpose through these works.

"Many more people must soon join together to imagine and envision good, in and for the world. In this way, they will work together to manifest good. Consider for a moment, that every manmade thing in your world was imagined first. Imagineering is a universal law. You cannot manifest anything you cannot first imagine.

"If you use your thoughts and imagination to appreciate—to express joy in having—the thing you envision, such as having a family of your own or a vocation that is helpful to others, the matrix is infused with energy until the only possible outcome is for the vision to become manifest.

"Keep in mind, this law applies not only to good and wonderful expressions. It applies also to fear and anger-based thoughts and visions. They, too, are available to all, forever. It takes longer for dark thoughts to manifest, but they do manifest, and thoughts that are full of fear have incredible power.

"As humans feed energy into their fears, the matrix can do nothing but respond to energetic input because it lives by energy and light. The more that is written in print about things like suicide and school shootings, the more people who know of them, the easier they are to imagine, and the easier it is for them to become manifest.

"You wondered about the difference between thoughts and written text. The more that is written on a topic, the faster the idea spreads to and through those who would have known nothing if they hadn't read the ideas, for example in newspaper articles.

"Much activation happens from a distance, through waves. When something on your planet is vibrationally loud, like a tsunami killing thousands of people, there is a ripple effect throughout the entire grid. First, there is the vibration of so many people, animals, and plants transitioning, dying, all at once.

"Then your media sweeps news of the natural disaster and ensuing deaths into millions of households around the world. The shift in the grid that is caused by the thousands of people reading about the event ripples throughout the entire matrix, aligning and realigning many thousands of liquid light-points.

Maddie was mesmerized by the images passing through her mind. Next, she was shown a man writing a newspaper article about HIV aid work in Africa and a woman in Nebraska who made it her mission to travel there and be of service. The woman would have known nothing of the problem if not for the newspaper story. The image in her mind showed clearly the moment the woman was activated by glancing through the article while standing in line at a Starbuck's. It was another inconsequential, daily moment that changed everything on the grid for hundreds or maybe thousands of people. And all of it came from that one newspaper article on a Tuesday morning.

The magnitude of changes caused by the tiniest daily acts overwhelmed her.

Reading her thoughts, Melchizedek responded, "Not everyone is activated so strongly, Maddie Clare. Some people come with very simple life purposes, such as to be great examples of love or to find love later in life or to set an example of maintaining a healthy lifestyle. Life purposes are unique. Different people are activated at different times; they are guided to the Illumination Station to be offered a new life purpose. The question is whether they will choose to claim it.

"Any change, shift, or vibration affecting the grid affects every person. This is why you must always be in a place of peace, gratitude, and appreciation—a place of love. Most people do not understand that movies, television programs, songs, and news that bring positive emotions into their home, heart, mind, and memory can make a change in their very life energy, their health.

"Be grateful, as simpler people have been. Be sure to bless all things you are ingesting. Be especially careful about your source of water (liquid). At this time, it is unlikely that your water comes from a loving or nurturing source.

"Consider the water you drank on the bus. Do you think it was packaged lovingly and gratefully by a family or community that loved working together? Was it put on the shelf lovingly and gratefully? Sold by people who appreciate their lifestyle? That's just one tiny, tiny example.

"Be sure you express your gratitude and love for each individual thing that enters your body. You should offer the words and emotion of gratitude in each thing you ingest. Express this prayer to all things you eat and drink.

> "I love you. I thank you and every single hand and every single entity that brought you to me. Thank you for the sustenance, the enjoyment, refreshment, and nourishment you bring to my life."

"Maddie Clare, this is your part of the grid, your work within the matrix. This is the life you were born to live and express. Your spirit chose this path long before you were born into this life.

I don't understand. What am I supposed to do?

"At this time, Maddie Clare, you are being called to remember who you are and to share your visions and discoveries. We ask you to share ancient wisdom, such as the importance of being reverent toward and grateful for the abundance of the Earth and for each day and each breath and each moment with loved ones. We ask you to reignite the section of the grid that was vibrant when humans lived in alignment with their appreciative, holistic nature. You have seen some of this in your visions. You have written of this in the messages in your journals."

She couldn't contain herself. "Who is we?"

"I speak on behalf of the high council of angels. We have tasked ourselves to protect children until these laws of the Universe are revealed for them.

"Have no fear. You will be guided. Everything is unfolding, just as *you* intended. You once lived in this ancient temple, scribing the vibrant light of the Maya, recording their teaching and knowledge in the scrolls.

But your life as a scribe was not your only human life, and today will not be the only time you are activated to illuminate a section of the grid.

"Remember, Maddie Clare … Remember …"

Wait! Melchizedek don't leave me here.

His essence was gone.

CHAPTER 8

Maddie jumped at the touch on her shoulder. She whipped around, and her hair hit Lynda in the face.

Oh my God, I'm out!

"Maddie Clare, where have you been? Everybody's been looking for you." Lynda's eyes demanded an answer *now*.

Maddie grabbed for her necklace.

Still there. Thank God! But where are my binoculars?

She could feel Lynda's unwavering gaze. "I … uh … lost my necklace. I was looking for it. Why, what time is it?"

Her eyes scanned the face of the pyramid.

Where was I in there? Where's the door? Didn't anybody see me vanish?

"It's twelve-fifteen. We've been looking for you for an hour—*everyone* has been. If we aren't on the bus in fifteen minutes, they'll leave without us." Lynda's voice was infused with annoyance.

I can feel her energy. I can almost see it ... like a colored vapor.

"I'm sorry, Lynda," Maddie was sincere but also distracted. She stole a glance back at the pyramid.

No way am I leaving tomorrow.

"Let's go, Maddie Clare! Come on!" Lynda said.

Maddie quickened her pace, but she slowed down again when she remembered her Nahual's folder at the woman's shop.

"Maddie, come on! The bus driver gets fined if he doesn't run on time, and he's already waited fifteen minutes extra for you!"

Shoot. Maybe they can mail it to me.

"Sorry. I seem to be kind of messed up today." She matched Lynda's pace and let the rhythmic shap, shap, shapping of their sandals soothe her as they jogged to the parking lot.

Lynda spotted the bus and turned in that direction. "They're still there! Come on!"

They ran across the parking lot, and the bus door opened. The driver gave them an annoyed look and jerked his head in the direction of their seats. He wasn't the only one annoyed. The disgusted looks on a few of the passengers' faces communicated their exasperation.

I'm glad they don't say anything.

Maddie brushed away a rolling droplet of sweat. A few passengers looked away then, satisfied knowing she'd run to catch the bus.

"Here," the priest said, handing Maddie a sandwich and a bottle of water. "I think you might be ... hungry?" His look was a bit too piercing, and she noticed the pendant cooling.

She took the sandwich, mumbled a quick thank you, and hurried down the aisle.

It wasn't going to be that easy. "Did you enjoy your day at El Castillo?" he asked.

"Ya … it was good." She pushed past him, toward her seat and her friends. Though he fell silent, his eyes implored her.

Can he tell something happened? Can everyone tell? Do I look like I've seen a ghost?

When Dani saw her, she said, "Jeez, Maddie, where have you been? We thought you'd fallen into the cenote or been sacrificed to the gods." She chuckled, but her annoyance hung in the air.

"Yeah, Maddie. What happened? Where *were* you?" Lynda echoed.

"I told you. I lost my necklace and went looking for it."

"You almost cost us a fortune for a necklace?" Lynda prodded.

"One minute, you were looking through your binoculars," Dani said, "then I turned around, and you were gone! I mean gone!"

"I must have bent down to look for the necklace, right at the time you turned back around. I'm sorry, you guys! I didn't ditch you on purpose."

Apparently, that was enough. They let it go.

"By the way, Maddie Clare." Dani grinned at her, holding up a white folder, "I picked up your Nahuals chart from the shop."

"You did? Oh, thank you!" Maddie exclaimed, reaching out to receive her treasure.

That was today. Today. *Feels like a week ago.*

She looked at the folder, gently opening it to reveal charts filled with teal-blue hieroglyphs, the mysterious symbols of the Maya. She tucked it into her tote bag, careful not to bend it, and looked up to see if the priest had noticed. Apparently, he hadn't.

Thanks for that, God.

Only when Maddie noticed people passing their phones around, sharing their Chichén Itza photos did she think to look for her phone. It was in her pocket, right where she'd left it, but her binoculars still hadn't reappeared.

She turned to face the window and opened her sandwich. When she stole a glance in the priest's direction, she found his gaze fixed on her. She held the sandwich closer to her face to shield him out. When she finished it, she busied herself fishing in her bag for an apple she'd stashed from the morning snack box. Anything to escape his gaze. Eventually, waves of exhaustion swept her into a fitful sleep.

She woke up when the bus rumbled over a speed bump, with a half-eaten apple still in her hand. She knew they were near the hotel, and so did other passengers, who started shuffling around. As the bus slowed to a stop, Maddie prayed nobody would talk to her.

I need a shower—and a drink.

Her mind drifted back to the pyramid, and the enormity of the messages she'd received. She choked back the lump in her throat and felt her face flush.

What am I supposed to do with all of that information? I can't leave tomorrow! I need to know so much more.

She tried to recall whether she'd actually *taken* the flight insurance or only considered it. With her head against the window, she opened her flip phone and scrolled through her emails. At last she found it: World Travel Alliance $29.95 flight insurance. She clicked the link, hoping she could make out the details on the tiny screen.

This might have been the best decision of my life, taking this insurance.

Maddie coughed and rubbed her chest, hoping Lynda might notice.

"Hey," Lynda said, "you're not getting sick, are you? We fly tomorrow."

Thank you, my friend. You can vouch for my illness.

"I'm not feeling right. Maybe too many late nights. I might try to stay an extra day or two." Maddie continued to scroll through the insurance details.

"How would that work? You wouldn't stay here by yourself, would you?" The concern in Lynda's voice was unmistakable. Like a great mother bear, she couldn't imagine leaving Maddie behind.

"Well, I won't be alone. The resort is full, and everybody speaks English. It will be easier to call off sick from work if I stay down here. Besides, isn't Dani staying awhile longer?"

Dani chimed in, "Yeah, we're here one more day."

Lynda pleaded. "Please promise me you'll travel back with them. I don't want you trying to get through the airport on your own."

Maddie fought the urge to remind Lynda how often, and how far, she flew for her job. Lynda's tone revealed depth and concern as she asked, "What about dinner? Will you come out with us? Are you feeling well enough?"

"I don't think so. I need to call the insurance company and see what my flight insurance covers. If I *can* make the change, I'll have to schedule the new flight as well."

"Here. Take my iPad. It'll go faster on that than on your tiny phone. One of these days you should get a proper smart phone. And if you change your mind about dinner, we're eating at the Courtyard Café."

About then, the priest got off the bus, and Maddie felt a wave of relief.

Why does that guy bug me so much? Does he fit into this chaos somehow?

Maddie nodded to Lynda. "Okay, sure. I'll give you a call as soon as I finish with the airline." She stuck the iPad in her bag and followed Lynda off the bus.

"If I leave the room before dinner," Lynda said over her shoulder, "I'll crack the door open. If it's closed, we've already gone out."

"Perfect," Maddie said over her shoulder as she headed for the front desk. There she found ever-faithful Angela, who promised to get her an appointment with the doctor, so she could get a prescription or at least a note for her boss.

Since I am declaring the flu, it should be okay to have a ... hmmm ... a glass of red wine? Or does a shot of whiskey make more sense? Any saintly changes will have to wait until tomorrow. Anyway, Noah drank, and so did Hemingway. And look what they accomplished.

As she passed the bar, she leaned over and whispered to the bartender, even though nobody was paying attention. "I'll take, uh … Jameson, a double." She coughed a bit more—she had the flu after all.

When the bartender handed her the drink, she laid two dollars on the bar, already wishing she'd gotten the wine, flu or no flu.

I don't even like whiskey.

But the bartender was already mixing the next customer's cure-all. She picked up the whiskey and headed for the Blue Wing.

When she opened the door to her room, she enjoyed the magical, automatic light one more time.

Strange how this room felt threatening this morning but now feels like the safest place in the world. "You are never the same from one morning to the next."

She raised her glass. "To you, Melchizedek, oh priest of the Most High God."

Then she found the envelope that held her travel documents and dialed the phone.

The responsible thing would be to get on the plane.

No, Maddie. You have to stay and figure it out or wonder for the rest of your life what the heck happened.

"Oh shit!" she said as the recorded message was playing through the phone.

"Press 9 to repeat these options."

Listen up, Maddie.

Once Maddie got through the maze to an actual human being, she went through her story, remembering to cough for effect as she made the new arrangements.

I don't know what I think I'm going to find out, but I've got one more day to do it.

Next, she called the front desk.

444, what a great extension!

"This is Angela."

"Hi, Angela. This is Maddie Clare Owens. I worked it all out, so I can stay an extra day. I fly out Tuesday morning. You think the doctor can see me first thing tomorrow?"

"Yes. Our house doctor can see you at seven-thirty if it's okay for you. He will give you a prescription."

"Oh, uh—*cough*—that's great news. I appreciate your help on this."

"I already took care of your room for you, Miss Maddie, because I am off tomorrow. My cousin Marina will be here, and she can help you with anything else. She looks just like me, except a little taller."

"Angela, thank you. I don't know how to thank you for all you've done."

"It is no problem, Miss Maddie. Did you say you need the concierge?"

"Yes. I forgot I had mentioned that to you … it's a bit of a personal matter." Maddie's mind raced for a way to explain, without truly explaining. "Ah. I bought a necklace, and I think it is Maya, and I want to learn more about it. And about some other Maya things."

"You were at the Chichén Itza today, yes?"

"Um, uh … yes. I just have a few more questions."

"Yes. I understand. I will call my cousin and ask her, so she can check around for someone. Sometimes there are guides who can be hired to tell you all about the Maya. She will have someone for you by the time you finish with the doctor."

Cough. "Thank you, Angela. You've gone above and beyond the call of duty this weekend."

"You are welcome. Have a good night and safe travels. I will have the desk call you in the morning, just to remind you of your doctor's appointment."

"Thank you again, Angela, and good night."

Desperate as Maddie was to take a shower, she really wanted to get Lynda's iPad back to her, so she could come back to her room and soak in the tub and contemplate the day. With that, she grabbed the iPad and headed out the door.

Drop the iPad, get a sandwich, hit the ATM, grab a beer ... or maybe a wine, then early to bed for me. God, I can't wait.

Lynda's door was open a crack, "Hello?" With relief, Maddie tiptoed in. She didn't really want to have a long conversation and didn't want to discuss her feigned illness. She opened the iPad and pulled up the notepad. "Thank you for everything, Lynda. I am flying Tuesday morning. I can go to the airport with Dani and Reed. The insurance is covering. Love you, MCO."

Maddie backed out the door and closed it quietly. Walking down the hallway, she noticed the breathtaking ocean view from Lynda's wing.

Guess being mother of the bride has its privileges. Good for Lynda. She deserves this.

As Maddie hurried down the stairs, she nearly ran into her goddaughter. "Kenz! I've hardly seen you all weekend. You feeling any better?"

"I know. Right? I was really looking forward to catching up. How was Chichén Itza?"

The nasal sound of Kenz's voice told Maddie she wasn't feeling great. But there she was, concerned whether Maddie had a good time.

She will be a great social worker, saving the lost souls of the world. She's beautiful inside and out. I hope she knows that about herself.

Snippets of Melchizedek's words returned to her.

Every moment has the potential to change everything ...

She knew that no matter her short-term plans (a drink and a sandwich), what she really needed was to light her beautiful goddaughter's area of the grid—and her own. The place where she and Kenz intersected in this brief moment.

"What are you doing right now, Kenz? You busy?"

"Not really. I was heading back from Dani's room to go pack."

"Do you want to sit on the deck for a minute and take in the breeze?"

"Sure!" The excitement in Kenz's voice told Maddie she'd made the right decision.

They each took a chair on the pool deck. Maddie glanced around for a waiter, but it was just her, Kenz, and the stars.

And that's just fine. This is more important than a drink.

"So. How's your life?" Maddie asked feebly, realizing she knew very little about her goddaughter these days. They lived too far apart, and they both had busy lives.

"Oh. I have no life. I've gone from being a poor student to being a poor wannabe social worker, struggling to get a job. I'm thinking about working at

Home Depot until I can find the real deal." Though her words were a bit depressing, her tone wasn't.

"Home Depot, eh? Your Mom is right, always saying how much you and I are alike. I love to remodel and restore things. And I love hardware. Will you cut me a discount?"

Before Kenz could answer, Maddie's voice grew soft. "You know. I did that. I turned away from what I loved, just to get a job. That was over twenty years ago. Especially after today's visit to Chichén Itza, I wish I'd followed through on my career in archaeology. I could have been exploring the temples and Maya ruins. Who knows? I might have found the secrets of Chichén Itza."

"You could've been on the cover of National Geographic," Kenz said, laughing.

"I'm serious, girl. You are a bright and beautiful young lady. If you love counseling, you should find a job you love and go for it! If you don't find exactly the right thing *right now,* that's okay. If you have to get a job at Home Depot for now, that's okay. But don't stay there. Don't turn away from your heart's passion."

Kenz nodded, obviously taking Maddie's words to heart.

"If something about your job hunt isn't working, stop and figure out what it is. Maybe you're trying to work with adults when you should be working with kids, or maybe you're trying to work with people who are recovering from accidents, rather than people who are fighting depression.

"Whatever it is, you'll know. Figure out which piece is missing, rather than dumping the whole thing—or worse yet, doing something that isn't right for you. That will only make you an old woman, looking back at what you missed. You're too amazing for that, Kenz." Smiling, Maddie sensed the grid lighting up.

That was five minutes, Maddie Clare. You devoted five minutes to love and grace, and behold the shifts in the matrix, the space created for an empowered MacKenzie. Remember this lesson.

"You might be right," MacKenzie said. "I will definitely think about that."

The ocean breeze was soothing, and Maddie felt herself nodding a bit, but she wanted to impart one more thought. "You know, sometimes when we choose our careers, we forget our priorities."

"How do you mean?" Kenz asked.

"Just as important as what you do for a living, you should imagine the life you want to live. What time do you want to wake up? What clothes do you want to put on? Where are you going? Who are you seeing? People almost never consider this aspect when choosing a career, and it's so important. In your case, maybe you are meant to teach at the college level, and you're just struggling through these first years to get to that place.

"I guess what I'm saying is when you're thinking all this over, don't think—*What job can I get?* Or, *how much money do I need?* Think about where you want to live and what kind of lifestyle you'd like. Think about who you want to spend your days with."

Maddie bolted upright, "Oh my God! I forgot Maybelle! I forgot to call the dog sitter to say I'm staying another day. Holy hell!"

"Oh, no! You'd better go make that call, or she will develop abandonment issues. Then she'll be coming to me for doggie counseling."

That Kenz, always taking time to make others feel well. I could learn from her.

"Seriously, Kenz. I love you. You're beautiful … And I've got to run and get my dog care sorted out."

"I love you too. I'm so glad we got to spend a minute together." Kenz stood and gave Maddie Clare a hug.

As they touched cheeks, Maddie hugged her a little bit tighter and whispered, "You're my family, you know?" Then she hurried on. "Safe travels. I'll see you stateside."

"Good night," Kenz said. "Oh, hey, I'll let Dani know that you want to ride with them to the airport."

"Thanks, Kenz. I appreciate it. I would have forgotten. Have a good night." Maddie knew she had done the right thing—for both of them. The grid had shifted, and Maddie knew this was true not only for them but for the world.

Nothing will ever be the same, even after that short exchange. Even if the ripple effects aren't visible, everything will be just a tiny bit different.

Maddie opted to take the long route to the Blue Wing—the beach. Maybelle could wait another minute. One more time, one last evening, she stepped onto the beach. Soft waves called her to take her place in the sand by the light of the waning moon. She sat down and slid off her sandals.

Now what?

She stared at the sea, waiting for a voice to answer.

A little direction would be good, right about now.

The only response was the gentle sound of the waves.

Well, I guess it's on me to decide how I shift my grid, but I have no idea what to do with tomorrow. How will I keep my promise to help the children? And who is the "one who is lost"?

The image of the priest flashed in her mind, but she brushed it away as quickly as it appeared. She wrapped her arms around her legs and rested her chin on her hands. Within minutes, she felt herself nodding off again. She had to get up now, or risk sleeping in the sand.

Maddie stopped at the bar long enough to grab a cold turkey sandwich and a mini-bottle of wine. "I don't suppose there's any way I could get a couple of these?" she asked with a sheepish smile.

"Sure, miss."

"Thanks." She laid a five-dollar bill on the table and put the wine in her purse. Halfway down the hall, she opened the sandwich and ate as she walked in the moonlight. Somehow that felt less lonely than eating in her empty room.

She recalled the night she first said "yes" to Cancun and how she had envisioned finding love, fame, and fortune. She could never have imagined things the way they had happened.

When she got back to her room, she slipped off her shoes and cracked open one of the little bottles. Despite the wave of exhaustion, Maddie desperately needed a shower. She opened the taps and reached for the fresh bottle of lemon verbena shampoo. Soon, the fragrance embraced her.

Melchizedek—Light Carrier—Keeper of the Universe. What could all this mean?

She finished washing off the day's grime and felt a bit revived. Fresh and clean, Maddie filled the tub for a soak, squeezing a bit of shampoo into the stream to build up some bubbles. With her stash of wine at hand, she slid into the soothing water.

She felt like she needed a plan for the coming day. After all, she had told the illness story to her friends, her boss, and the insurance company. That white lie couldn't be for nothing.

Maybe I can find the old woman from the market and she could answer some questions—like how she found me and why she gave me the necklace. Maybe she could help me figure out the colors and temperatures. I could even ask about the teleporting thing—how she disappeared in the market and how I went from outside the pyramid to inside.

How are you going to find her Maddie Clare?

I could look for her at Chichén Itza, like the driver said. That way I could also check out the other structures—The Temple of the Jaguar and the Temple of the Descending God. I can see if anything activates me.

Activates you, Maddie Clare? To disappear again? With a one-on-one guide, that would be tough to hide, and even tougher to explain.

Maybe I will stay a little closer to the hotel and just ask the guide to help me understand my Nahuals.

The plan was settled. Maddie closed her eyes, intending to just breathe and rest for a moment.

Light Bearer. Scribe. Channeling the Ancients. Illumination Station.

She began to nod in the comfort of the warm, lemony soak. She jerked her head up when her chin hit the water.

She climbed out of the tub and pulled the plug, imagining the tensions of the day oozing down the drain.

If only life were that easy.

Bits and pieces of the message rolled in and out of her mind—*other hidden scrolls, Keeper of the Universe, masters at bending the light, messages will come to you, this room will be discovered.* Maddie thought back to her early automatic writing experiences.

I was picking up thoughts and messages from the grid, even though I didn't realize it at the time. That explains why the images and early visions were silent. I was just picking them up in a nescient way. When I began to ask questions, and complete dreams using the visions, and hear things, then I was actually opening the channel. I've got to get home and read that book Ruth gave me. Now it makes sense, "for your journey." I didn't realize she meant literally, "read it on the plane."

Her mind searched decades of memories, trying to think where she had put the journals filled with automatic writing. Were they in her apartment? In storage? At her parents' place? Or had she simply thrown them out at some point, thinking nobody would be interested?

As she slid between the sheets, she couldn't imagine anything feeling fresher. She laid her damp head on the pillow.

I wonder what awaits me tomorrow?

PART III

THE ADEPT

CHAPTER 9

A handwritten note, addressed to "Maddie Clare Owens" was taped to the door of the hotel infirmary. Maddie looked around.

Dang it! I need that prescription for the travel insurance and my job.

The note read, "From the desk of Dr. Emilio Rojas."

Great! Dr. Red!

A chuckle escaped her. She glanced around to see if anyone had heard it, but the corridor was empty. The rest of the note was in Spanish, but she could decipher *Recepcîon del Hotel.*

Maybe he left the prescription for me at the front desk?

The man behind the desk smiled warmly as she approached. "Buenos, señora."

After reading her little piece of paper, he exclaimed, "Ah, yes! We have a package for you." He disappeared behind the counter and then popped back up, with a white paper bag in his hand. "Here you are!

This note is from la Señorita Angela. It is in Spanish. Would you like me to read it to you?"

"Yes, please."

"The doctor has made you a prescription in the bag, with a note that explains your illness. La Señorita Angela says don't worry. The prescription is very light. You can take it for a mild headache or not."

"Okay, thank you." Maddie reached for the bag.

"There's more. She says her cousin, la Señorita Marina, will not be in until eleven o'clock today, but she has arranged a guide for you. This man is very well known for his knowledge of Maya ceremonies. He will come to this desk for you at eight-thirty."

"Thank you. Ah ... Muchas gracias, señor. I appreciate you reading the note to me." She took the bag and asked, "Did Angela leave the name of the guide?"

"No, ma'am. She only says he will be here in about ... one hour. I think she is speaking of el Señor Martinez. He is known for assisting our guests with questions and taking them to ceremonies to experience Maya spirituality. I think it will be him."

"That's great! I'll get some coffee and be out here."

"Yes, ma'am, claro. I will have them bring coffee to you."

"Thank you, señor. Cream for the coffee, too, please. Thank you for everything."

"Sí, señora. Buenos días."

Her demeanor turned happy and hopeful.

Maybe this Señor Martinez will be able to answer my questions about how I got inside that pyramid. Or was I inside it? Was I teleported, like Captain Kirk? Or like the woman in the market?

A pepper-haired gentleman appeared with coffee and steaming cream. To her surprise, he also set down a small plate with two strawberry crêpes.

"Oh. Thank you, señor. Muchas gracias."

Mindreading takes luxury service to a whole new level!

"De nada, señora. It is my pleasure." He hovered not far away, where he could easily hear her (or perhaps read her mind) if she needed something more.

I could get used to resort living—if I can get it without pyramid encounters and apparitions in the night.

The chuckle only lasted a moment before her more pragmatic self stepped in.

What will you do with these visions, encounters, and biblical characters, Maddie Clare? You are an accomplished insurance adjuster! Are you really going to give that up to become the Psychic Channel? Or maybe you think the dinosaur energy in your necklace will work with your Calvin Klein suits and your all-business office. Just where do you think all of this is going?

Hmmmph. Nowhere right now. Right now, it's strawberry crêpes on the beach in Cancun. In a little while, it will be a research outing with a Maya guide. Maybe I will even find the old woman.

She took the pendant in her left hand, saying, "My Dear and Loving Angels and Guides, light my way to the old woman. Give me the guidance to walk my Divine path."

After the prayer, Maddie gave the pendant an extra squeeze, whispering, "Where is she? Can't you find her for me?" Then she refocused her attention on the melting whip cream that covered her crêpes.

Best enjoy this moment, Maddie Clare.

She held each bite of strawberries a moment on her tongue to take in their full decadence. After the last bite, she considered asking for a second plate—she wouldn't be getting this kind of service tomorrow—but she was already running late to meet Señor Martinez.

Leaving her $2 tip on the poolside table, she hustled to the lobby. As she neared the front doors, she noticed a heavyset man at the front desk, standing with his back to her. The Galactic Butterfly was getting warmer against her chest.

She had just opened the door when she heard the man say, "Miss Maddie Clare?"

Oh my God! It's the priest ...

The pendant cooled. Eventually it was like ice against her chest. "Uh, hi there. What a ... coincidence. I didn't expect to see you here."

"Really?" he approached her with his hand open and guided her to one of the lobby chairs. "I understand you would like someone to answer questions for you about the Maya—and perhaps about Chichén Itza? You must be feeling better today, yes? You have better color in your cheeks."

Again, his look was a little too direct for Maddie's comfort.

Did I tell him yesterday my name was Maddie Clare? Or did I just say Maddie? Did I even tell him my name at all? Maybe he got it from Angela's cousin or the front desk.

"Um, yes. I was asking to know a little more about Maya spirituality. You know, the history and maybe some of the practices ... But they told me it was a Señor Martinez who would be coming for me."

I certainly can't tell him what happened. There's something ... off about this guy. Why does he keep looking at me like that? Maybe he knows something.

"Ah yes. That is my name. I am Renato Martinez."

"Oh. Sure. What about ceremonies? I didn't see any at Chichén Itza."

"Well, yes. Sometimes there are ceremonies there. Would you like me to take you back there to make a ceremony?" The slightly giddy tone in his voice made Maddie Clare uneasy.

"No. I mean, that won't be necessary. I saw Chichén Itza yesterday, and it's a long way. Maybe something a bit closer?" Absentmindedly, she reached for her necklace again.

"Oh, you are still wearing the Galactic Butterfly. It is very beautiful. I know a closer place where they make many ceremonies. Going there will help you understand some things. Today is a special day in the Maya cosmology and a good day for ceremony. Shall we go there?"

"Uh. Well. That's ... very nice. Very generous of you. Uh ..."

Go, Maddie Clare! You stayed the extra day for this very reason. You have angels watching over you. What could go wrong?

"Okay. Let me just tell the front desk where I am going in case the doctor asks for me. Can we leave your cell phone number?" Her voice was weak as she tried to hide her discomfort.

155

Darn Midwest upbringing. Always be polite!

The priest handed his card to the man at the desk and said, "I will be taking Miss Maddie Clare to Mis Palmas for a small ceremony."

"You are very lucky, señora. To go with such a high priest as Señor Martinez is a great honor. You must be very happy."

This guy seems to like him. Maybe he's the real deal. Melchizedek was a high priest, too.

She could only manage an "Mm hmm."

I can see the headlines now, "Woman With No Life, Found Lifeless in Cancun." Ha.

"So, what did you think of our Chichén Itza? It is a very special place for the Yucatec Maya."

"Really? What makes it special?"

Maybe he'll tell me what I want to know without my explaining everything.

"It is one of the oldest ruins here on the Yucatan Peninsula. It was a great center for commerce and ceremony in its time."

"What kind of ceremony?"

"Ah. Here is my car," he said, gesturing toward a hunter-green Gran Torino. "Let me just put a few things in the back."

He opened the passenger door, swept a few things into a pile, and unlocked the trunk. When it opened, Maddie Clare saw big, black, boom speakers—so big, there was barely room for his things.

That's odd.

Then she noticed the black plastic trash bags. She shivered, again thinking of the ghastly headline— "Lifeless Woman Found."

I must be out of my mind. I could never explain this to my dad.

"Get in," he commanded happily as he hurried to the driver's door. "This is my nephew's car. Mine is in the shop, with my supplies for the ceremony in its trunk. We will make a quick stop to buy new supplies."

"What kind of ceremony will it be?" She clasped her hands in her lap, wishing fervently to be anywhere else but in that car.

"Today is our Day of Justice. It is a good day to recognize right from wrong and equality from inequality."

"Okay … You mentioned there were also ceremonies at Chichén Itza?"

"Ah, yes, the sacrifices. At Chichén Itza, they sacrificed humans into the cenote. The cenote is a clear water-well fed from underground. People from many long distances needed the cenote to provide their drinking water so they could survive."

Her mind flashed to the image of still water, red with the blood of children.

Drink that? With blood in it? That can't be right.

"You are cold, Miss Maddie Clare?"

Her necklace was icy. "No. I am okay. Just a chill. How far is it to where we are going?"

"Only another fifteen minutes to the market. I wish to buy some things for this ceremony and then it will be some few more minutes to Mis Palmas."

As trees flew past the car, Maddie Clare noticed very few other vehicles and none on their side of the road.

Wherever we're going, looks like we'll be the only ones.

She leaned her head to the window, not because she wanted to sleep but because she wanted to widen the space between them. Then she looked at him squarely. "Señor Martinez. I think yesterday you mentioned they sometimes sacrificed children?"

"Ah yes. Unfortunately, they often sacrificed the children, especially girls who were not yet mature for marriage … and making babies."

He must mean their first period. That's around the time the visions stopped for me. Maybe that's not a coincidence.

He pulled up to a roadside stand that was barely more than wooden planks and a corrugated-tin roof; no sign of electricity. The young girl inside looked like she should have been in school.

"We have arrived. I can tell you more of this after I make some purchases. I will get you a bottle of water Miss Maddie Clare. You must not get dehydrated."

Maddie Clare was thankful for the opportunity to hop out of the claustrophobic vehicle.

I wonder if I should offer to pay?

Hanging from the rafters were single-string-wicks with a slim candle at each end. The priest picked out a number of them, in various colors, along with two glass votives, like the large devotional candles many Catholic churches have on their altars for pay-for-prayer.

We must be making a Catholic–Maya ceremony.

She tried to keep the chuckle—and her skepticism—to herself.

The priest pulled a few bills from his pocket and said something in Spanish that Maddie could not make out. The girl produced two books of striker matches.

Shopping done, Maddie and the priest climbed back into the car. As they turned back onto the highway, Maddie reminded him, "You were going to tell me about the sacrifices at the cenote. Why did they sacrifice children? Who could do that?"

"It is difficult to explain … In that time, everything depended on the harvests and storing enough food to get through winter."

"But winters are mild down here."

"Yes. To you they are mild. The sun feels good and it is true it is warm all of the year. But like anywhere, there is a time when crops grow and a time when the land rests. Here the land rests in the hottest part of the year, instead of the coldest."

Okay. That kind of makes sense.

"There were many ceremonies in those days—to the sun and the rains and the seasons. This is why ceremonial places like Chichén Itza were created, not only to study the stars and the calendar, but to make ceremonies for what was necessary to live. The priests and priestesses of the time lived as kings and queens because they knew how to make the ceremonies. Many sacrifices were for ceremonial reasons, but sometimes sacrifice was used for personal or political reasons, while being declared part of the ceremony.

Maddie tapped her fingers on the armrest. "Are you saying they murdered children for personal and political reasons?"

"No, not the children. Not usually."

Not usually?

"During that time, it was believed that if enough tension was created in the Universe, it would force the gods to bring what was needed. Loud noise was thought to create this tension, like when warriors yell and scream while rushing into battle.

They sacrificed the children because the screams of innocents were believed to be especially powerful. The screams had to be *real*, too, not fabricated to manipulate the gods. They needed the children's screams to bring the rains after the hot dry season."

"Clearly," she muttered.

Hoping to calm the rising disgust she was feeling, Maddie took a swig from her water bottle. "What about their parents?" she asked. "No parent would allow their own child to be thrown into a well."

"You are right. The parents did not bring them. The priests and priestesses created a system. A group of young men, who yet had no children, became known as the Gatherers. The Gatherers would disguise themselves, round up a group of children, and chase them to the cliffs above the cenote. They knew where the children would hide in the jungle because they had hidden there when they were little.

"Normally, the first children would not see the edge coming. They would fall, screaming, and most fell to their deaths. Any child who survived the fall would be trained as a priest or priestess. That was a very good thing for the child's family."

"What about the children who didn't fall off the cliff—the ones who saw it coming and turned away? Or what if too many children survived the fall? How many priests and priestesses could there be?"

"This is where it gets interesting. The children who survived the fall and became priests and priestesses recognized those who had turned away because they had all been chased together. Up to five of these children could be chosen by the new priests and priestesses to be scribes or assistants. You might think of them as altar boys. Usually, if more than one fell from cliff and survived, they would take the one with the least injuries to become the priest or priestess, as it showed the greatest miracle.

"Of course." Maddie shook her head, trying to get more air.

"Remember, children were chased and sacrificed like this only for certain ceremonies. At most, this happened four or five times in a year."

Scribes? I was a scribe! When I fell off the cliff, I must have survived!

Maddie begged her mind to retrieve images from her nightmare, but she could only recall bits and pieces. No matter how she tried to bring up the image, the tension in the car prevented it. So, she continued to hammer the priest with questions.

"Didn't the chasing guys know the children from their community? Somebody had to be a cousin or an uncle or something."

"First, you must remember these young men had been chased themselves as children, and they managed to escape. Yet they were not chosen to be scribes or assistants. Maybe they were angry. Even though their feelings were misdirected, maybe they were trying to get revenge. Is this not something like your 'bullies' in America?"

Maddie shot him a look that said, "Seriously?"

"The times were different. People knew this as the only way, so they probably did not question it as you and I do. Remember, this was a time when children often died, from fever, malaria, many things—

including sacrifice. If they survived the fall into the cenote, they became priests and priestesses. As such, they were very wealthy and honored in that culture."

Right.

Water wasn't the only thing she was going to need to cure her revulsion. "How were these men disguised?"

"They camouflaged themselves in mud and small sticks. For the most part, they disappeared against the trees."

Maddie's stomach hurled, her throat went dry, and she choked back a small cough.

The mud people. Here. They were real.

Her heart pounded, and her breath became heavy. She felt the Galactic Butterfly getting warmer on her chest.

Where am I going? Where am I going with this guy who's so unemotional about child sacrifice? What else does his "spirituality" deem as okay in a ceremony?

The road sound grew rumbly as they entered a gravel road. "Señor Martinez, is it much farther? This looks like the road to Chichén Itza. Didn't you say the place was close to the hotel?"

"No. The market was close to the hotel. Mis Palmas is a private ceremonial place, near to Chichén Itza, where we can make a sacred ceremony."

Her stomach flipped. A private place? A sacred ceremony? Like the ones of the ancient Mayas? What is sacred about sacrificing life?

Her face flushed red, and she tried to slow her breathing. Her finger began to tap the door rest, near the handle, as she contemplated she was going to be at this ceremonial place alone, with this man who had done nothing but make her uncomfortable from the start.

Ya. There is no way I could ever explain to my dad how I ever got into this car. I've got to get away from this guy. I wonder if there are taxis ...

Reaching into the back seat as he put the car in park, he produced her lost binoculars. "I found these at Chichén Itza yesterday. They are yours, yes?"

"Oh ..." Her jaw dropped, but she managed to retrieve the binoculars.

He must have seen me disappear in the crowd, like Dani, only he knew where I had gone.

"Miss Maddie Clare?"

"Yes, señor?"

"Did something seem familiar to you yesterday? At El Castillo?"

There it is. That's what all this was about. He knows.

Her voice took on a dry tone. "No, Señor Martinez. I've never been here before."

"I understand. Do *I* seem familiar to you?"

She stopped, dropping the binoculars into her bag.

He thinks he recognizes me. Let's get this over with.

She met his gaze with a steely look. "No, Señor Martinez. I met you yesterday—and again today so you will show me ceremonial things. Then you will take me back to my hotel."

Her voice commanded his actions would return her safely. They were not friends. This was a business transaction. She adjusted her bag crosswise over her shoulder, with the new weight of the binoculars inside.

Looking out the window, Maddie saw an older Maya woman on the ground near the parking lot, tending a fire. Seeing her made Maddie feel a little calmer, a little safer. In fact, numerous fires were burning around the parking area and around a small, open-air shrine. A closer look revealed the fires had been ceremonial. Flowers, corn, chocolate, and candles had been arranged to form colorful Mandalas. Then all had been set alight, creating smoke and flames in all the colors of the rainbow.

Desperately needing fresh air, she gathered her things and stepped out of the car.

I need to find a different ride back. There's no way I'm getting in a car with him again.

The priests and priestesses were offering up prayerful chants and blessings to the skies then dropping their heads in humble invocation. Looking around, Maddie was intrigued by the complexity of the ceremonies.

She closed the car door and walked closer to watch the flower rings burn. Her mind flashed back to the dance and chanting of Blue Snake Cloud.

I wonder which flowers make the smoke blue?

Taking a deep breath, Maddie Clare squared her shoulders and shifted into her stern, insurance-adjuster role.

You asked for a guide, Maddie. Even if he's weird, you're here to learn, and you paid him to teach you. Get going.

Maybe. But I still don't trust him. What if I hadn't called for a guide? Was he going to just keep my binoculars?

In a dry voice, she asked, "Señor Martinez, what are these people doing?"

"They are making traditional fire ceremonies, in which the Maya priest or priestess opens a portal, so the people can commune with spirits. Offerings are made to the fire and to the spirits. Remember, today is the Day of Justice on our calendar.

Before she could ask why today was related to justice more than any other day, the priest pointed to a ceremony taking place below a raised, stone shrine. The shrine was reminiscent of an abandoned altar. It reminded her of the abandoned structures she had seen in the brochures for Chichén Itza, with raised columns that had once supported a roof.

"Look, there. That is Don Michata. He is a renowned Maya priest who makes wonderful ceremonies. Even he recognizes this sacred place on this day. This is very good. This a day when we celebrate justice for all the people."

She noted Don Michata was wearing a white shirt, black jacket and pants, and a colorful purple head band with a matching cloth sash around his waist. The woman priestess wore a skirt, and Maddie could feel her indigenous spirituality in the brightly colored cloths that she wore. They reminded her of the stoles that ministers wore for Easter services.

I wonder how they *see this priest, in his blue T-shirt and cotton jacket. He hasn't even put on a dress shirt or tie. Do they see that as disrespectful? I wonder if it's his mix of education, Christianity, and Maya cosmology that make him seem so out of place.*

Maddie turned in a circle to get her bearings. The very tip of El Castillo peeked through the trees, showing Maddie that safety was nearby if she needed to break away. Still, her rational mind couldn't drown the call of her sixth sense, "Run! Get away from this man."

We are *at Chichén Itza. Why didn't he just say so? Priest or no, this guy is cagey.*

He led her across the parking lot, around and through the ceremonies, and past Don Michata. The priest veered onto a dirt path that led to the stairs, and like an obedient child being led to the principal's office, she followed. The smudgy scent of burning flowers, tobacco, and chocolate had an intoxicating essence, and she briefly wondered if she smelled a bit of *weed* in the fire.

Maddie looked up and saw a sculpture of a Latin American man in a purple robe, with a gold cross around his neck and another at his waist. He had a black padre hat and a snide mustache. She immediately thought of Don Novello's "Father Guido Sarducci" on *Saturday Night Live*.

What? I know we aren't here to worship Father Guido. No way. I came here to be serious—to learn about Maya cosmology.

Maddie noticed bottles of what looked like whiskey on the steps up to the shrine, along with pennies strewn about. For a moment, Maddie eyed the booze.

That could prove handy.

The priest must have noticed because he began to tell her of San Simon, the patron saint of prostitutes and money.

Maddie was dumbfounded. My angels must be laughing their wings off right about now.

"San Simon is a very special saint," he began, "protector of prostitutes and children. He is deeply revered, not only with my people, who call him San Maxîmon but in the Christian world, too."

Yea, sure. I've never heard of him. Maybe where I'm from he's known as Father Guido Sarducci.

Maddie chuckled at her private joke. Then, glancing around the open-air shrine, she started to feel maybe the whole thing was a sham for tourists.

How did the Maya people go from incredible feats of engineering and the creation of an accurate and sacred calendar to worshipping a guy who belongs on Saturday Night Live?

Weird! Maybe to you, Maddie Clare. If these guys are pretending to be reverent, they are doing a surprisingly good job. Besides, how did the Christians go from Baby Jesus to Santa Claus and reindeer pulling a sleigh?

Unable to shake the apparent contradictions in the scene around her, Maddie Clare dutifully bowed her head and lowered her eyes.

I just have to get through this and get back to the hotel.

The priests' prayerful chants faded, as some of Melchizedek's words and the absolute feeling of sacredness that took place during their time in the pyramid returned to her.

That was real and sacred. This is contrived. It feels like a sham!

She glanced around without raising her head.

"Now we make our ceremony for the Day of Justice." Señor Martinez held out his hand and guided her to a rectangular steel table on the vacant altar space.

He pulled out the bag of goodies from the market. She hadn't looked at them closely when he was purchasing, but it was clear he had chosen them carefully.

He explained that he would set up his ceremony to the right, and hers to the left, because the right was masculine and the left feminine.

So, how does that work when his client is a man?

He lit one of the larger candles and used its wax to heat the base of the others to stand them up in a straight row of thin red candles at the back of the table. He then made a matching row of red candles on her side of the table. As he used the hot melted wax at the base to stand them on the steel table he began his explanation. "The red color represents the east where the sun is born and is considered to be the primary sacred direction."

Then a row of yellow candles—first his, then hers, yellow representing the south or the right hand of the sun." As he set the green candles, he explained, "This color is a green-blue and it is associated with the Maya concept of heaven, earth, and the underworld. It unites the four cardinal directions; it is like the center of a cube, though our world is round."

He positioned the white candles, taking extra time to set them in the right place. It appeared to Maddie that he was blessing each one as he set it. "The white candles represent the north. The side of heaven, because it is the direction from which the cooling rains of winter are born, as well as the direction of the North Star, which the sky pivots around."

Row after row, color after color—red, yellow, green, white, and finally, in the front row, black.

Black in the front, right next to the white, seems strange, but I guess he knows better than I do. Maybe that's the justice piece—black and white, good and bad, right and wrong.

"As he set the black candles, his language became a bit more pointed and staccato, saying "Black is the sacred direction of west and the dying place of the sun when it leaves us at the end of each day."

"Okay," Maddie said weakly. She looked up and down the rows on their table. The 50 slim candles were arranged perfectly symmetrically. Pursing her lips, she contemplated his last sentence and the strange ordering of the black and white candles together on the table. She noticed her pendant getting warm.

Huh. Wouldn't that make red and black opposites? Didn't he say the sun rose in the red color? The east?

As if you knew anything about Maya ceremonies, Maddie.

Ya, but wouldn't the opposite of black be white? Meaning the sun should rise in the white rather than the red? I've clearly lost the plot here.

"Now we are set up, and we will begin our ceremony. I will make a prayer and light my candles. Then you will light yours. During the lighting, only the Maya incantation should be said."

His intensity was unmistakable as he commanded, "I will say it for us."

The priest began a soulful display of incantations, sometimes looking down, pausing in a hushed prayer, and other times raising his tone to an aggressive pitch.

Aggression at injustice toward children, I hope.

The priest lit the red candles, on his side of the table, starting in back and working from the inside out. Then he nodded to her to light her red candles from the inside to out. Obediently, Maddie lit them all.

169

Well, this is kind of cool, actually. I have to admit I'm a bit curious.

The exchange continued. The priest first lit his row of one color and then motioned for her to light hers. After the row of white candles, the priest took one of the big Catholic candles and lit it, then said a prayer, lifting it above his head, as if presenting it to the Lord Himself for approval.

Maddie glanced around and noted similar ceremonies behind them on similar tables. As she looked around the structure, she noted she was the only white female on the altar space.

Señor Martinez lit his last row, the black candles. From the inside to the outside, all five candles, completing his side of the table.

Great. We are almost done. Maybe I'll grab a few gifts at the market before getting packed up.

She had not felt a single spiritual surge, wave of excitement, vision, or dream. Nothing.

"Miss Maddie?"

"Yes?"

"It is your turn. You must light your last row of candles." His tone was both commanding and expectant. He watched her closely as he tapped his fleshy fingers on the altar-top.

"Oh yes. Thank you." Maddie took the packet of striker matches and lit the match. As she touched the match to the inside black candle, it went out. She took another match and lit it, but when she touched the wick, it, too, went out. "Huh. That's kind of weird."

The priest gave her a long look, "Don't you embrace your dark side?"

"Clearly not," Maddie muttered, without thinking and without intending to say it out loud. "I mean. No. I don't embrace my dark side."

What's he talking about, my "dark side"? Didn't the black candles represent a setting sun just a minute ago?

"We must all embrace all the parts of our soul— both the light and the dark. Otherwise we are denying an aspect of ourselves and allowing our ego to think we don't have any weakness ... and we all have some weakness."

His words were heavy, ominous. His face darkened.

She continued to light match after match. She only had two left when the priest said, "You have to light those candles. You cannot leave this ceremony unfinished! It will bring great trouble!" As his voice rose, a few of the other Maya priests and the old woman looked up. A few people stepped closer, watching the exchange intently.

"I'm trying!" Maddie's voice was anxious. Nobody wanted to get out of there more than she did. Besides, here was this priest inferring that she was "doing it wrong" because she was not lighting her dark candles. What she wanted to say was, "You bought them! You set them up. If they don't want to light, that's your fault!"

Since she was to her final striker match, the priest handed her one of the votives. She lit the large white glass candle without any trouble. Then she tilted it to use as a lighter for the black candle closest to his, which she noticed were firmly ablaze. She carefully held the black candle in the white candle's flame for a few seconds and then drew it back. The black candle went out.

His voice rose, "You must embrace your darkness, Miss Owens. Weren't you raised Catholic? You know you must confess!" The word, *confess* echoed across the structure, and the other practitioners fell silent.

Catholic? How does he know I'm Catholic?

Still the momentary images of the pitch-black confessional, on her knees, with a priest imploring her deepest sins from the other side of the screen came to her. Her hands shook as she felt the *fear of God* for the first time in her life.

I have to finish this. And get out of here.

She lit the second black candle with the big white one. It promptly went out. The priest shot her an angry look, his face a grotesque blend of darkness and red, sweaty palpitation.

As if it's my fault, Mr. Maya Priest. They're your damn candles.

Perspiration dotted her forehead, and her hand shook as she balanced the glass candle and tried to light the third black candle, knowing she was now out of order. She felt the priest's angry gaze bearing down on her. Glancing up, she saw his face—and his energy— had turned beet red. She glanced around, hoping to steady herself. Instead, the other priests and priestesses were all staring at her and slowly approaching the structure.

Oh my God, Maddie. Light the damn thing so you can get out of here. You don't know these people. This could get dangerous.

With that realization, she began to sweat and pinched the inside of her cheek between her teeth. The priest took her arm, his strong fingers gripping her just above her elbow. Leaning into her face he hissed, "Do you remember me now?"

From the distance she heard the distant tribal echo of "Ya'ax muyal kan."

"Blue-Snake-Cloud."

The pendant scorched her chest as she shot a terrified look back to the priests and priestesses behind her. They were gone. Their colorful burning mandalas emitted thick sooty smoke into the air, but there was not a soul in sight. She pulled her arm back but couldn't get free.

"Please, I don't know why you're doing this."

The sneer in his face turned vicious and for a moment Maddie was transported back into her nightmares of the triumphant sneer of a muddy face at the edge of the clearing as she started to fall.

Yanking back from his grasp she looked up to the forest and saw the camouflaged outline of men against the trees.

Oh my God. No!

Maddie's eyes flew open wide, and the glass candle fell from her hand, crashing onto the stones. Jerking her arm free, more candles fell to the stone altar.

She ran blindly across the ceremonial space, tripping down the steps. She knew she would have to choose between the parking lot and the jungle paths. She spotted a white trail into the jungle, certain it would lead to El Castillo.

Not far behind, the priest called out, "Wait! Miss Maddie Clare!"

She ran faster than she ever could have imagined. Her long skirt tugged at her body and tore, as the outstretched arms of trees reached for her. There were no tourist barricades here. Her breath wheezed from the heat and the effort, and eventually she stopped, leaning on a tree to catch her breath. And to listen …

She could no longer see the pyramid or hear the priest steps, but before she could catch her breath, she heard movement behind her—many feet tramping on the path and in the jungle. She glanced back.

The mud people!

Fueled by terror, Maddie felt the branches brush and scratch her face as she surged forward. Frequently looking over her shoulder, she saw them behind her. Even running as fast as she could, there was no way to diverge from the path. The walls of the jungle trapped her.

This is how they killed my friends.

Her head drooped, and she knew she couldn't run much farther when she saw the impossible—the clearing. Finally, the jungle was opening to the light, and she would be able to see El Castillo. She tried to yell, "Help! Help! Anyone. I'm an American! I'm being chased."

But she had no voice. She was in no shape to run like this.

As she finally reached the clearing, she tried to get her bearings to the pyramid, but she'd only gone about six more steps when she saw the cavernous opening in front of her.

My God! The cenote!

Wobbling on the precipice, she knocked a couple of stones loose. They fell—tikety-tik—down the face of the cliff. Dropping to her knees at the edge, she gasped for breath.

The rustling sound behind her signaled that the mud people had arrived. She hunched her shoulders and closed her eyes tightly, waiting for the stab of a spear or hands pushing her off the cliff.

"Wait," she said in a hoarse whisper, as she turned on hands and knees, her feet sticking out over the edge of the cliff. She faced her attackers. Expressionless, mud-masked faces looked at her from the edge of the trees.

How is it they aren't panting? Or even sweating?

She looked back over her shoulder, certain her life was over. There was no fight left in her. She couldn't even cry out. But then, when she turned back again, the mud people were receding into the jungle, their camouflaged bodies fading into the trees.

What the hell? Am I too old to be a suitable sacrifice? They chased me all the way here? What stopped them from forcing me over the edge?

Trembling, she pushed herself up from her kneeling position. Stinging pain came from a scrape on her arm. She looked all around her, desperately hoping the mud people had seen another person that made them back away. Her eyes made out white stones indicating another trail to her left, and this one had a tourist barricade.

Maybe I should call for help. Surely somebody would hear me, but maybe it would be the priest. Too risky.

Shaking, she got to her feet and started for the new path. Soon, she saw the pinnacle of El Castillo above the tree line.

This must be the right direction.

A small creek trickled out of the jungle at the edge of the trail and proceeded to make a steady stream of water down the side of the cenote. She knelt alongside it to rinse the scrape on her arm.

She held her breath to listen long enough to determine she was alone. Then she splashed her face, tossed her hair, and opened her mouth to the sky, whispering, "Thanks, God." Regaining some composure, she leaned forward, putting her hands on her knees to stand. It was then she caught a glimpse of her reflection in the water.

Looking back at her was the young woman from her visions and dreams. Maddie spun around, certain the young scribe was behind her, but she was alone. When she turned again to the water, the young woman's expression was calm, as if to say all was well in the Universe.

As Maddie brushed hair from her face, the young woman did the same.

My soul reflection? Is that possible?

The distant sound of a car interrupted her musing. She stood and hurried down the white stone path.

CHAPTER 10

Maddie knew better than to step in front of a moving bus, but she had to take the chance. As far as she knew, the priest was still looking for her, or—worse—this could be the last bus. When bus door opened, it was Manuelo, the driver from the day before. Taking in Maddie's appearance—her scraped arm, torn skirt, and scratched and dirty face, he motioned for her to find a seat. The other passengers' faces screamed, "What the hell happened to you?"

Maddie was thankful when a young girl got up to let her sit down. Her legs trembled, as she climbed into the seat. The little girl handed her a packet of "personal wipes."

Realizing she must look like a disaster, Maddie chuckled and thanked the girl. The girl's thirty-something mom must have thought the same. She called her daughter to come sit on her lap and handed Maddie a bottle of water.

With a concerned look, the woman whispered, "Are you okay?"

Maddie said a breathless "Yes, thanks," and began to clean her scrapes with the wipes. Perhaps the woman thought Maddie's appearance was the result of a fight with a boyfriend or some other drama Maddie wouldn't want to share. Whatever she thought, Maddie was thankful she asked no more questions.

Refraining from gulping, Maddie drank the bottle of water in less than five minutes and stared out the window.

What the hell just happened? Divine Guidance? The Grid? Holy God, what a mess! I will never know what happened here. Why in the world would the universe send me that priest today of all days? Justice my ass!

Maddie took a deep breath. She reached for the knots of her necklace and carefully loosened them. Pulling the necklace from her neck, she stared down at her pendant, knowing she was praying the impossible prayer.

> *My dear and Loving Spirits and Guides, lead me to the answers I need—to safe haven—and let me find the old woman from the market to guide me.*

Her grasp on the necklace loosened just a bit as her head tipped forward and sleep overtook her, with the pendant in hand.

When the bus hit a speed bump, Maddie woke and looked up. They were back to the highway stretch of Riviera Maya. When she spotted the familiar international flags that signaled the Grand Oasis Tulum Resort, she thought of how a hot shower would make her feel purified from this very dirty day ... and the dark side. She returned the Galactic Butterfly to her neck and cinched up the knots to tighten the fit.

Home! Sort of, anyway. And home to Maybelle—really home—tomorrow.

Directly across from the hotel, Maddie noticed four or five stands boasting colorful rugs and woven fabrics. She needed to get some gifts for family, so she signaled the driver she wanted to get off the bus. Along with gratitude, she gave him the $50 she'd brought for her "guide."

Then she exited the bus and hurried across the highway. The priest's question taunted her, *"Do you remember me now?"* Maddie regretted ever asking for a stranger to teach her. It was a stupid risk to get into a car with a total stranger in a foreign country. While the messages in the pyramid had been amazing, they were not distinctly Maya. Besides, the Maya had already proven themselves to be a bit ... *unpredictable* ... what with their ceremony of casting children to their deaths.

Who did that priest think he was? Who did he think she was? And the Day of Justice? What the heck did that have to do with her? Why did she hear the Blue-Snake-Cloud chant?

She stopped in her tracks, wondering if the priest had been the one who was already lost, like the old woman had said. Then again, it was a riddle, "Two of you are on the path. One of you is lost."

Her very soul wrestled with the gravity and strangeness of the statement. It sent a chill down her spine though she couldn't be sure what—or who—it referred to.

"Two of <u>you</u> are on the path. Hopefully, that indicates I'm one of the two. And if we're on the path, with the other one "lost," then maybe for us, the two, there's no other possible outcome.

Most important, is the priest one of the three? He definitely recognized me. If he's one of the three, which one is he, and who is the third person?

Finally making it to the other side of the highway, she stopped at the first booth. The crafts were colorful, but they all seemed a bit touristy. She wanted something a little better for her shopping list recipients. Something that spoke of the beauty of the Maya people and their culture.

She touched the fabrics absentmindedly, feeling weary and craving the refuge of her room. But she wouldn't be able to explain to her family why she went to Cancun for five days without bringing something back for them. She straightened the pendant at the base of her throat and tried to focus on the task, but her brain continued processing the day.

I still don't understand what happened yesterday. Why did Melchizedek come instead of a Maya? And now I don't understand today either. What is the deal with the mud people?

As she picked up a green, jaguar-headed blade, the young girl behind the counter beamed at her. "You like, señora?"

"No, thank you. Uh … Gracias, no." To be very clear, Maddie shook her head.

It's so difficult saying no to those imploring eyes. Is that because I was once a Maya?

Maddie hurried away from the vendor and cast a glance down the highway. If she didn't find something at these four booths, she'd have to walk half a mile to the next one.

That's not happening. It's a shame my flight is too early for me to shop at the airport. Home! Oh my God! Maybelle!

Digging in her purse to find her cell phone, she felt a gentle touch on her arm. She jumped a bit and swung around to find the old woman who had given her the necklace.

"Oh … oh… it's you. I …" Everything that had happened to her came flooding back. She couldn't help the tears that were welling in her eyes. She couldn't keep herself from telling the old woman everything about the events of the day—getting into the car with a stranger who declared himself a Maya priest, the candles that wouldn't light, being chased through the jungle. The words tumbled out faster and faster, as the woman with the gold-edged tooth listened patiently, nodding and holding steady her knowing, accepting expression.

"And … uh, the black candles wouldn't light. He told me I *had* to light them. I had to embrace my dark side! And then the mud people chased me. I was sure I was going to die!"

Oh my God. This poor woman. She probably didn't understand anything I said. She must think I'm some American maniac."

"My child, what were you doing, trying to light *black* candles?"

She speaks English! Thank God.

"It was his idea! I didn't know any better! When they wouldn't light, I knew there was something weird, but I didn't know what he was trying to do or why he had me involved in it."

God Maddie Clare, you sound so lame. Victim, victim, victim! It was his idea? Get over it, girl! You got in the car!

"My child, you cannot *be* what you are *not*. Black candles are not for you." Her English was perfect, and Maddie wondered where she'd learned it.

"There is more?" the woman asked gently. Maddie looked down at her sandals, now dusted in the white clay of the street. "Did the priest comment on your necklace?"

"Not specifically—but, yes. He also asked if … if he seemed familiar to me … if I remembered him. He seemed to have an agenda. And, yes, there is so much more." Maddie Clare glanced around to a few people watching her and the older woman. "Can we go someplace more private?" She didn't want to be standing at a highway market where he could drive by anytime.

Thank God this woman is here. Is she the one who is keeping the commitment with me?

"You can come to my church. It is not far. Just a few streets."

As she fell in line behind the woman, who was now leaving the market, Maddie asked, "Your church? I thought you were Maya? Are you Catholic too?"

"No. I am Presbyterian, in fact, but I am also a Maya priestess. Here it is possible to be Christian and believe in the Maya cosmology. While I am an elder in the Presbyterian church and in the Ecumenical community, I am born and raised a Maya priestess first and foremost. Here we experience both.

"You *cannot* be what you are not, and you *must be* what you are. For me, this means that if I make any criticism against another, it is visited back on me ten times. This is part of the *nature* of me. And as is true with all nature, one cannot alter it. It is law."

As Maddie listened, a wave of relief poured through her body.

A law. That's what Melchizedek spoke about. This woman makes sense to me.

"We are here."

"Where is this?" Maddie asked. The door they came to looked unlike any church Maddie had ever seen. It was steel, with ornate metal in what would be the window. She tried to peer in as the little woman unlocked the gate.

"It is my home. I do healing work here with herbs and prayer. Many women come here in the afternoons to learn, to pray, to have healing, and to celebrate life. It will be some time before they arrive, so we should light a candle." She turned with a grin that seemed to encompass her entire body. "But no black candles. No more black candles for you."

The chuckle was soft, and she turned and shuffled away, waving a hand at Maddie to take a seat in the courtyard. Maddie looked around. The courtyard was light and simple, with herbs growing in pots and a table with two wooden folding chairs that didn't look too sturdy. Maddie continued to stand, straining her ears for any sound of the old woman.

She appeared in the open doorway and beckoned Maddie in. Though she felt the relief in being here with this woman, her senses were still on guard. "Excuse me, but what is your name?"

"Ah," the woman said, grinning. "I am Doña Rosita. I am a Maya priestess."

A priestess who gives away necklaces in the market?

Maddie's open mouth and confused face must have urged Doña Rosita to go on.

"I was trained in the ways of the Maya priestess from my earliest days. I was tasked, as part of my purpose in this lifetime, to introduce the true Maya cosmology together with all faith and so I trained to become a Christian minister as well.

"Sometimes, I am shown the face of a person who will come to me for guidance. Sometimes these are people who are to become Maya priestesses?" The question couldn't be missed, but Maddie Clare ignored it, as if she didn't understand its implication.

"Your face was shown to me last year—that you would come. I was to give you the Galactic Butterfly necklace in the market. Then you would come here, and I would give you information."

At last!

"What information?" Maddie could not hold back her excitement.

"That part was not fully revealed—only that I was to give."

"That's it? Are you kidding me?" Maddie hadn't intended for her voice to turn sharp, but overwhelm prevented her from controlling it. She needed answers, and she felt like the sun was going down on this adventure.

"Before we begin, we must set a prayer for protection, to create a safe and sacred space. That is always the first thing. Without it, other energies can enter."

The woman pulled back a woven curtain, which revealed a small closet-like space. A wooden sculpture hung on the wall above a table covered in a white cloth. On it were seven or eight Maya sculptures made of unfired clay, along with a few candles and fresh flowers. There were high windows, right next to the ceiling, and Maddie couldn't shake the feeling that this was, or had been, a clinic of some kind.

The woman turned to the table and chanted in a low voice, using a language Maddie couldn't make out—certainly not Spanish or English. Then the woman turned to Maddie Clare and took her hands.

The old woman's hands were warm and soft, like a baker's hands, well-oiled day after day and year after year. The woman lifted their clasped-together hands and moved them left, right, forward, and back, as if in an ancient ceremonial dance. The movement soothed away the tension Maddie Clare had been feeling.

Doña Rosita. I must remember all of this.

Doña Rosita's volume suddenly increased. Though her words sounded angry, her energy was not. It was more like she was calling to a higher power.

I wonder which higher power she calls? Jesus? God? Mary? Maybe even Maxîmon, like the priest? God, let's hope not. I wonder if she knows the priest— but because of her "nature" she couldn't say anything critical of him. Strange they're both priests for the Maya and the Christians.

When Doña Rosita finished speaking, she turned to Maddie Clare and gestured for her to sit down. "Now, we must talk. Tell me of your experience."

"I'm not sure I know where to begin. I booked a tour to Chichén Itza. Everything seemed normal. Oh, actually I have to go back more. First, there was a dream."

"Ah yes. That is good. The dream will be important." Maddie told her of the blue smoke, the people in the fields, and the chanting of the Blue Snake Cloud. Doña Rosita began to hum the exact melody of the chant ... Blu-ue-ue-ue Sna-a-a-ake, Clou-ou-ou-oud.

She knows the song from my dream!

She looked in Maddie's eyes, "I know this song. It is a special ceremony for the time of rest after the harvest, when we place faith that our harvest is complete and sufficient to carry us to the next one. Through the time of planting, through the summer rains and dry times, to the time when we will receive again. It is very important to end all harvests with great reverent ceremony. It is something like a memorial—honoring of life, saying goodbye to the field of plenty, wishing good journey for the next phase of eating what we have harvested."

"Huh. Ya. I hadn't thought of it that way."

Maddie had never thought of anything that way. In Beaver Lake, people were relieved when the harvest was over. Spring and summer were stressful months.

"Okay. Then there was this ... *thing* ... an apparition kind of thing that came to my room and was breathing on me. It was ... uh ... big ... Just a head ... no body or arms." Doña Rosita closed her eyes as if she were looking for something in her mind. "It kept moving around my face, looking at me. It didn't hurt me or say anything. But right after it left, there was an earthquake."

"Ah, B'atz." Doña Rosita said the word as if she had seen it. Just like she had plucked the Blue Snake Cloud Song from Maddie Clare's dream, she seemed to have plucked the apparition out of her mind as well.

*I wonder if that's like a Vulcan mind-meld? She just hooks up and—*voila!* Or maybe she's picking up on something from the necklace. Or directly from the grid. Is that possible?*

"Ahh. No. It wasn't a bat. It was like a Maya thing."

Rosita's laughter startled Maddie. She had been so busy recalling and thinking she hadn't realized she had also closed her eyes.

Jeez'. Did I just fall asleep?

"No, not bat. B'atz is the Maya symbol for life, destiny, and infinity. Here in the Yucatec Maya world, he is known as Chuwen, though I still call him B'atz, as that was his name in the south, where I grew up.

"He is the Maya god of creation." She paused as she pointed to a round ceramic wheel mounted to the wall. It had two layers of symbols and what appeared to be a man in the middle with a great weight on his back. The images were the logograms in the style of the Maya glyphs.

Maddie looked at the ceramic wheel closer.

Hmmm. That long macabre mouth with the huge protruding nose are quite like that thing that hovered above me in my hotel room.

"The god B'atz created the earth and the sky, life and wisdom on the Maya calendar wheel. He represents the nine months it takes a child to develop from conception to birth. This cycle of birth repeats itself in many things. So, for example, if you start a new business, B'atz may arrive and it will take nine months for it to be born."

She lifted one eyebrow and said, "To have B'atz visit you, especially when you are not practicing Maya religion is ... *significant* ... and something to be grateful and happy for."

"Wait a minute. Are you saying I am going to be creating something? Like in nine months? I don't know about that but now comes the big whammy ... As I started to say, I went to Chichén Itza. That's actually where I met the priest. He was our guide on the bus. When we got to the pyramid, El Castillo, I went to ..." Maddie suspired as she prepared to share her tale.

Here we go. ...

She exhaled forcefully again, biting at her lower lip. "Okay. We got there, and my friends and I were at that pyramid when I saw this door. A ... a steel door, something like the front of your house but more like bars. Like a jail door. I was looking at it. I was looking up the stairs as the guide was telling us all about the pyramid. But he didn't mention the door."

Thoughtfully and gently the older woman nodded her head, saying, "Yes. I know this door."

Maddie went on. "Then I looked up and thought I saw some symbols." She pointed to the calendar wheel. "You know, like those over there. And, well, I saw one that looked a bit like my necklace, so I was trying to pull at my necklace to see it when all of a sudden ..." Maddie held her breath as she again fingered the necklace. "Uh ... I was inside the temple. Doña Rosita, I was *inside* the temple—El Castillo." Her voice had dropped to an excited whisper, as if someone might overhear. Doña Rosita's face displayed the same warm, understanding expression she'd had all along.

Nothing surprises this woman! Or she was there. Watching you.

"Carry on." She nodded. "I understand." The woman sat patiently, as though they had a million years for this conversation. Maddie couldn't tell if it was getting dark outside. The lighting in the room hadn't changed since she entered.

"Um. So, do I tell you everything?"

Another patient nod.

"Okay. There was a woman's voice at first, telling me about … about … myself. She told me I had been a Maya girl, a young woman, working inside that pyramid as a scribe. Children were being sacrificed, and I could hear their screams as I worked. I wanted so much to save them, but I couldn't. I vowed to come back."

Her words were coming faster and faster, but the old woman continued to listen and nod.

"Then there was a man's voice. He said his name was Melchizedek, a name I recognized from the Bible." Doña Rosita's thin smile widened just a bit, nudging Maddie on.

"He told me how the Universe works, how things come into being and how they interact. He said there is a matrix like a totality of many interconnected grids, holding all the information for all time. I'm not sure I can remember or repeat every detail. It was so much information. But he made it sound like there would be more … *strange things* coming in my life. He was right, and I didn't understand any of it. So, I decided to stay another day. I wanted to find someone who could help me understand, but I ended up with that priest instead."

"Mm, hmm … perhaps you two had some unfinished business from another time." She let the meaning of her words sink in. All was happening as it was meant to happen.

Then she went on. "Now let me tell you about the Galactic Butterfly, which we sometimes know as the Grandmother–Grandfather Butterfly. This symbol, the one on your necklace, was not originally Maya. The version you wear on your pendant came to us from another culture, and various cultures have embraced different versions of the image over the course of all time.

"Imagine if I said to you, 'Draw God.' Perhaps you could draw images or examples, but you can't draw God. Some people use light or sound or color to represent God, but there is no image that you can say, "That is God."

Maddie could only imagine music—some angelic song—to portray God.

"An image was created that you may have seen and is known as the Maya Tree of Life, and it was similar to the one on your pendent, but it did not have the swirling motion, which helps to describe the continuous flow and circling of time and cycles. It also didn't have the black and white imagery that you would see in the Yin and Yang symbolism of duality and wholeness. And last, it did not have the antennas reaching out in the four directions to receive and broadcast information."

Maddie touched her pendant, willing her thumb to make out the image on the surface.

"If this image could only be three dimensional, you would see a center point, from which all emanates. The center point is the now, the present moment, or sometimes it is you. You are the center point in your Universe, in your life, in your moment—and that is what the Galactic Butterfly image tries to convey."

"Is that why it seems so much like a mood ring? It picks up the energy of the present moment?"

"More than an energy, the Galactic Butterfly is *the source*, the starting point and the motion of life. To explain it is like explaining God. While you have an image for Jesus, what image would be similar to God? When your pendant becomes warmer or cooler around certain people, places, and things, the Galactic Butterfly is picking up the energy of the surrounding intention. When the energy is a new beginning, the pendant is warm and lively and green. Death or the energy of ending produces an icy feeling. A spiritual intention or energy will manifest warmth and a golden color. Anger and rage bring red heat to the stone."

"The Galactic Butterfly is said to represent all of consciousness that has ever existed. This is all of our physical ancestors—human, animal, fish and plant life, as well as the consciousness that organized all of the raw material from a whirling disk into the stars, planets, and solar systems—all of the Universe as we know it. In many ways the image shows us the time before birth. The time of tensioning the Universe to manifest a new creation."

"Wow. You sure chose the right symbol. That is nearly everything Melchizedek spoke of. Then he finished and *whoosh*! I was back outside of the temple again. A lot of time had passed, and my friends were worried. We had to run for the bus. Then the priest was there again, watching me as if he knew where I'd been."

"Yes. I can understand. This is why it will be important for you to always say a prayer of protection."

"He taught me a prayer! Melchizedek did." Maddie bowed her head.

> "I love you. I thank you, and every single hand and every single entity that brought you to me. Thank you for the sustenance— enjoyment—refreshment, and nourishment you bring to my life."

"He said to be sure to say that prayer, especially before I eat or drink."

"Yes, reverence and prayer are activators for many things, and it is very important to always express gratitude. What I am speaking of is *protection*.

"Many energies and entities surround you, and other humans, but are not in a tangible form. So, it is important to set prayers for protection, especially for the times you are seeking more knowledge. This seeking can make you vulnerable to energies that are not working for your highest good."

Maddie felt a chill. *Is she talking about ghosts and those kinds of entities?*

"Do not worry, child. You are accompanied by very good, very supportive energies. Like B'atz there are many *normally-unseen* entities—you have read about angels and ghosts? They are very different from

B'atz, but they too are always around us. Some Christians will tell of experiences where they heard or saw Jesus. These are real experiences of an entity who chooses to be seen, felt, and heard. They always exist. They are always here. B'atz is another kind of entity, one we embrace in the Maya cosmology. He chose for you to experience him.

"Do you understand what I am saying?" Doña Rosita looked at her closely and waited for a response.

Suddenly it clicked for Maddie Clare.

"Oh wait. I get it! Just because a ghost or entity walks in the room, it doesn't mean I know they are there. They could come and go, without me realizing it." As she finished the sentence her mouth turned to a frown as it sunk in, just how utterly creepy that possibility was.

Ya. I definitely need a prayer for this.

"There is a sense you sometimes call the sixth sense, which is in operation when you *feel* something intangible—like when you *feel* that someone is telling you a lie, or you feel someone standing around the corner before you see them. You might call it intuition."

"Like when you get goose bumps or a shiver up your spine" Maddie interjected. Thankful to finally be able to contribute some sense to the conversation.

"Yes, that's it. Sometimes your sixth sense will notify you that a *presence* is near you or in your space.

"Because you cannot always sense the energies and entities that affect your life, you will want to protect that time and sacred prayer space, just like we did today, so only true and accurate information comes through. You don't want to give any undesirable entities an opportunity to feed you information suited only to their own agenda."

Seeing the look on Maddie's face, Doña Rosita said, "Don't be frightened, Child. Fear is an attractor. It adds another dimension of complication and can draw undesirable entities to you. Just say your prayer of protection and go on about your day."

"Okay. Can you help me? Is the prayer in that foreign language you were speaking earlier?"

"The specific language does not matter. Prayers can be said in any language because all words convert to pure intention. They are received accurately by Highest Divine Power, no matter which language you use. In the same way, you can call the Highest Power by whatever name you choose—*God*, *Allah*, *Goddess*, *Great Spirit* and so on. Here is the prayer:

> "Great Spirit. Guide me in my thoughts, words, actions and intentions this day. Heal me of any fear-based thoughts and bring your greatest and clearest direction to me. Give me clarity and light in doing that which is meant to be done by me. Allow me to see and receive messages that I may best serve myself and others for the highest good of all. Amen."

"*Amen*? Is that Mayan?"

"*Amen* simply means 'and so it shall be.' This intention can be expressed in any language All of life is expression and intention. You will learn of that later."

I'm still scared, whether I'm supposed to be or not.

"Doña Rosita. There was something else strange. The woman's voice in the pyramid said to me, 'Two of you are on the path. One of you is lost.' What did she mean by one of you is lost?"

The patient nod of the older woman conveyed a feeling of peaceful wellness and love in the Universe. "While the potential of your destiny draws you to it, the Universe actually only records things as they occur and as they pass. Because she told you *two of you will keep this promise* ... This means that you and one other still have every possibility of fulfilling this Divine commitment that you made."

Maddie thought she noted a shift in the twinkle in Doña Rosita's eyes.

I'm thinking it's you who's keeping it with me, oh sly priestess of the ancients.

But Doña Rosita simply went on, not showing her cards.

"*One of you is lost* would imply that one of the three has turned away from this promise, willfully. And because of this, that part of their journey—that turning away—is already written. It is something like when Peter denied Jesus three times. If the third person chooses to return and fulfill the promise after all, that will also be written. Until the last breath of their physical life, there is still hope. But their history will always include the turning away. So, you see, '*One of you is lost*' ... so far."

A wave of full understanding swept over Maddie. *Now I get it!*

"So ... now what?"

"I believe there is one more thing you have yet to tell me. You spoke of some mud people chasing you."

"Ah, yes. When I was a child, I received what my grandmother called 'visions.'"

The woman nodded her head. "Go on."

"At first they were magnificent images of things I had never seen or touched. It felt almost like a game. As I got a bit older, the visions became almost interactive. I could think about an image, and a scene would begin to play out before my eyes. The visions enabled me to finish a dream when I was awake. They were great." Maddie smiled.

"And then …?" the old woman urged.

"When I was still a young girl, I had a nightmare of being chased, and it wouldn't go away. I couldn't finish it in a vision, and I couldn't stop it from coming at night. Eventually—either by force of my will or because I was growing up—the visions stopped. Much later, in my 20s, I began to do some automatic writing, which was a similar experience.

"In fact, the automatic writing was something like having Melchizedek or the voice of the older woman coming to my room and speaking to me, but without teleporting me, or ever showing themselves."

"Of course, because then your story would be all about what they looked like, rather than the information they were channeling to you," Doña Rosita interjected.

Huh. That's just what Melchizedek said. Where did this woman come from? How did she know her own path so well?

Pushing back to her explanation, Maddie Clare continued, "Even though I'd had some nightmares and dreams recently, I hadn't had a vision for several years until coming here. I guess if I think about it, each time a vision started to happen, I stopped it. I pushed my mind to intercept it, so I wouldn't have an uncontrolled vision."

"Mmmm ... and how are they now? Here in Chichén Itza?"

"The visions, dreams, and experiences have been everywhere. First in a dream with a girl running with scrolls in her arms, and then being inside the pyramid with Melchizedek and today with the mud people." Her pitch climbed higher, and she choked back a tear. "Today they were there, the mud people. They were at that altar place with the priest and they chased me all the way to the cliff above the cenote. I was sure I was going to die."

She paused, and her voice calmed a bit. "But they backed away into the jungle and stopped there. When I stopped at a creek to wash my face, I saw the young woman, the scribe, looking back at me through my reflection in the water. I could see the difference in our appearance. She was young enough to be almost boy-like, but I could tell she was female. Her face was calm." Maddie paused.

"You know, it was as if she was the calm, the knowing that should be in the very heart of me. This thing Melchizedek told me I must remember. I must remember who I am. But that reflection knew exactly who she was ... and she is me ... Or ... I am her?"

"Your soul reflection," Doña Rosita said. "The reflection of the human life your soul lived hundreds of years ago. Some people can see these in other people, but it is a rare gift of awakening to see your own soul reflection. It means you are changing your station in life. You are waking up and will walk the world of the messenger. The Light Carrier.

"You have been a channel, picking up the messages. You have kept them close, playing with them and learning how to interact with them—sometimes with your mind and sometimes in writing. Now your station in life will change. You will be a messenger. A Light Carrier of truth."

I guess we will see about that ...

"Doña Rosita, can you tell me about the seventh sense? You mentioned the sixth sense. What is the seventh?"

"The seventh sense involves color and light." The old woman walked away, and Maddie stretched her neck toward the doorway, but could no longer see her. A moment later she returned with an unfired ceramic figure. It looked like a deer with antlers holding the sun in its arms.

"Here, I have something for you. I am being guided to give you this gift to help protect you on your journeys. He is called Grandfather Manik here in the Yucatan and K'ej in the language of my youth. He is another of your Nahuals. He represents the four directions. You will travel the earth in your life purpose, and he will protect you and bring you greater awareness on your journeys."

"'Nahuals?' I got this folder from a woman at Chichén Itza, but I have not had time to look at it. It's a beautiful teal watercolor on parchment, with a four-by-four quadrant of figures and a page-wide image at the top that I could not fathom, but it looked like the entity B'atz that visited me. Do you know what that is?"

Maddie felt deflated, exhausted by her own ignorance. She lamented all the time she had wasted in her life, reading sappy romance novels and partying, when she could have been learning these amazing things. Even studying archaeology and ancient cultures. Her face flushed.

"I will not get into the long details of the Nahuals now because you have so much new information, and in truth one could spend many years studying this. Nahuals are in accordance with the Maya calendar of thirteen weeks and twenty days. They are like astrological signs and zodiac charts, telling much about the life you came to live. Suffice to say that much like your zodiac, there is a single, simple-sign for the month and day of your birth, but if you went to see an astrologer, they could give you much more information.

"When I read an individual's Nahuals, I normally take two or three days to prepare. I make prayers and ceremonies, and I look at their personal Tree of Life, which includes four more tones to the basic birthdate. The report you purchased at Chichén Itza most likely refers to B'atz because it references the Maya long calendar and the nearly two million days that passed between the calendar's first day and the day of your birth."

Two million days? How would she know that? I have to go look at that folder.

"You were born to unique Nahuals. You came to be the storm—to change things up. You were born into a secular life, an average North American, but you were not meant to stay there. You were meant to have this sudden realization ... this knowing of many universal truths. Another aspect of your Nahuals references heaven on earth. Brown and blue eyes also have this meaning, especially that splash of blue at the top of your brown eye. It is very distinctive." She looked into Maddie's eyes and smiled.

"You will bring many universal truths to the earthly plane. You have come here to live an extraordinary life—to communicate with the ancients and to deliver that sacred knowledge, in understandable language, to the people of the earth.

"Are you sure? I'm about the least saintly person on the planet."

The woman's eyes twinkled. "It is okay, child. You will understand over time, and the fact that you grew up with limited understanding will make you a better teacher. Others will relate more easily with you, and you will relate more easily with them. This is how you were meant to come to this moment in your life; all is as it was intended.

Gingerly, Doña Rosita wrapped the unfired figure in a long sheet of paper from the table. She placed the package into a unique kind of wrap and tied it closed. "Now, you must take Grandfather Manik for your journey—for you to create protected space and to place on your prayer- altar."

"Altar?"

Doña Rosita's face beamed as she held forth the Grandfather sculpture, and as Maddie reached out to receive it, she noticed her own hands looking fragile and small. She took the package in her hand and felt a tingle throughout her body. Inexplicably, all the exhaustion of the day was replaced by invigoration.

Wow, how do I accept this sacred altar piece without understanding it? Is it going to teleport me somewhere with no idea of how to get back, like the necklace did?

Doña Rosita said, "You must just *feed* it once in a while. Appreciate it with the gift of chocolate or flowers, and it will always be there to protect you."

Oh wow, a rule. I guess everything of great power has them—or should. I sense it comes with more responsibility—more weight—than she is sharing with me. Is it a false god? A golden calf?

I still don't know much about the messages of the woman in the pyramid, the message from Melchizedek, or these universal laws. Am I just supposed to go back home and return to work?

The older woman's words interrupted her again. "Things will be different now. You will come to remember who you are and why you came to live this life. Why you were adopted. Why you grew up on a farm. You will come to know all things."

"How will I know what to do?" Maddie asked. "You've had years and years of training. You know about these things. You have … tools, spiritual tools."

"As do you, dear child." The look of compassion and encouragement had returned to the woman's face. Maddie saw she was expressing pure love, along with confidence in Maddie's abilities.

If only I could feel that way …

Maddie handled the sculpture as gently as she would a newborn baby, still unsure what she was supposed to do with it or exactly how to care for it.

Doña Rosita led her to the courtyard door, just as the first woman arrived for prayer and study, and

Maddie wished she could join them, to have more questions answered.

"Have no fear, child. Teachers will appear as you come to each universal lesson. Do not fear what you do not understand. Melchizedek will continue to come to you with messages and insights. You must only go about your day doing what you do."

Doing what I do?

Once again, the energy drained from Maddie Clare. She looked to Doña Rosita for insight, but her face still held nothing but pure love.

Maddie wrapped Doña Rosita in a long, tender hug, wondering if she would ever see her again. Then she stepped outside the steel door, closing it softly behind her and turned to find her way back to the market before the sun set.

CHAPTER 11

The few concession stands were still vibrant and active, with vendors trying desperately to get one last sale. Maddie Clare did not disappoint them, quickly picking out placemats, purses, and jewelry, along with a few candles for her altar at home.

Not that I have one—but I will.

The sun sat low in the sky as she crossed the highway to her hotel. It was time to start packing.

She pushed on the revolving door, and the man at the front desk looked up and gave her a friendly wave. She walked over to check for messages from Dani and Reed, or the airline. She felt much more than a day had passed since she had picked up her prescription that morning.

"Ah, yes. Here is a note for you from Miss Dani." Maddie took the piece of paper, which was folded, as if for privacy.

Hi, Maddie. I hear we are traveling together tomorrow. Please meet us in the lobby at 3 a.m. to catch the taxi to the airport. We are in room 222 if you

*need anything, but we will be going to bed very early
to get up for tomorrow. Love, Dani.*

She glanced around the lobby while the desk
attendant checked for other messages, and once he
confirmed there were none, she headed for her room,
passing the bar with no thoughts of drinking. She
wanted to turn in early, too.

At the café she grabbed some fresh fruit and a
handful of sandwich meat and cheese. Then she headed
for Room 308.

Sliding the key in the lock, she wondered if she
would find any ghosts, or entities in her room.

*Home will be dull compared to all this. How can I
just go back to my old life as an insurance adjuster?*

With a deep sigh, she set her packages on the
bureau, exhaling from every cell in her body. Then she
took three long, soothing breaths. Exhaustion was
catching up with her again, and she worried that if she
fell asleep, she might never wake up.

Fighting to keep her eyes open, she forced herself
up and bustled about the room, folding clothes and
laying things out for morning. She set the alarm on her
phone and on the clock radio for 2:15 so she would be
on time. Then, as she pulled back the sheets and set a
bottle of water on the bed stand, she idly reached for
the Bible.

She started to flip back to Hebrews, hoping to read
about Melchizedek.

Why did you pick me?

But the thought had barely passed through her
mind when the Bible slid from Maddie's fingers, as she
dropped into a deep slumber.

The alarm jolted her awake with a loud and festive Spanish melody. She bolted upright, excited for the day ahead and the travel back home. Amazed at how restful her sleep had been, she sat on the edge of the bed, stretching her arms high, arcing them from side to side.

Wow! No entities, voices, screams, dreams, apparitions or holograms. Only sleep, blessed sleep.

She hurried through a quick shower, tossed her remaining items into her bags, and hustled to the lobby. She glanced to the bar—not for liquor, which she had all but forgotten. Her only thought was for coffee. Seeing there was none, she stumbled through the darkness toward the door.

She passed the lobby chairs, finally coming to the last one, where she found Dani's husband, Reed, stretched out and snoozing. She tiptoed past, so as not to wake him, and headed to the front desk to get a receipt for the insurance company.

"Yes, señora?" It was the same young friendly-faced man from the day before. "You are leaving us today?"

"Sí, señor. It is time for me to go home."

"I hope your trip with el Señor Martinez was a good one?" His curiosity was obvious, but she put an end to that line of conversation.

"It was interesting, thank you. May I have my bill please?"

"Oh, yes. Oh, and there is a note here from the airline. They had to switch your seat on the plane. They would like you to stop at their desk when you arrive to the airport."

"Of course."

Just then, Dani walked up. "Hey. The taxi's here. Are you ready to go?"

"Ya. I've got everything. How about you guys?"

"Yep. We're all set for a nice three-hour nap to the airport."

"Sleep time for me too," Maddie said.

The cab was a minivan, with plenty of room for them and their bags. Maddie Clare kept her bag with the new altar stone in her lap. Thankful for the darkness, she settled in for a snooze.

"I know you can hear me Little One, though you are asleep." It was the woman's voice from inside the temple. "I will tell you something important now, and when you see the rainbow, you will remember these words.

"Your life will be different now. More signs, symbols, and entities will come to you to reveal lost and forgotten truths. They come to reignite sections of the grid for you and others to discover.

"You must remember your promise to help the children. This promise must be fulfilled. You must live the life that you were born to live. You will be protected, but you must also be prepared—for the next adventure, for the next knowing. In every lifetime you have been a keeper of universal secrets and truths. This life is no different. You must remember, Little One."

When the cab hit the first speed bump, Maddie sat up to discover they were in the city, and Reed was already working out the tip with the driver.

Soon they pulled up to a building as impressive and ornate as their hotel.

This is the airport? How did I miss that when I got here?

The driver pulled their bags from the van, while Maddie said her goodbyes to Dani and Reed. Then he sent the young couple to their airline before turning to Maddie Clare. "Who are you flying with today, miss?"

"Oh. I'm with Gotta-Go Air. I need to stop by their desk.

"Ah, yes. It is up that escalator, second desk on the left."

"Thank you. Muchas gracias, señor." She shook his hand, hoisted her carry-on over her shoulder, and wheeled the other bag behind her.

The Gotta-Go logo loomed red ahead of her. Five or six people were in line, and Maddie took her place, pulling out her papers and passport. Finally, the woman waved for her to approach the counter.

"Good Morning, miss. Buenos." The woman smiled warmly and accepted Maddie's papers and passport. Then she slid a blue and white customs document across the desk. "You will need this at the top of the escalator when you depart."

"Oh. Thank you. I understand there was an issue with my seat?"

"Yes. Your new flight did not have the same seat available, so we have moved you. Now you are in seat 1D, at the front of the plane. We hope this is no inconvenience."

"Ah. No inconvenience. Thank you."

First class! If this is one of the "new experiences" Doña Rosita spoke of, I can easily get used to this.

The woman stamped the documents and waived her hand for Maddie to follow the escalator to customs. Maddie was anxious to get through the paperwork and find a cup of coffee before her flight. She walked by the closed shops, glad she had taken the time to shop at the market.

At last she spotted a place that served cappuccino and stepped forward for a coffee and biscotti. She inhaled deeply as the barista steamed the milk, eagerly awaiting the morning's delicacy.

The hour passed quickly, and soon Maddie joined the line to board the plane. Indeed, the counter-lady had been correct—1D, front row window. With no space under a seat in front of her, Maddie put her carry-on in the overhead.

I guess you will ride up top today, Grandfather Manik.

The sun was already bright at six-thirty in the morning, and everybody got settled in as the stewardess went through her safety routine. Maddie glanced about, checking her surroundings in the front seat of the new airbus.

Don't they offer champagne or something? Do I look like a person put into first-class due to lack of space rather than a wealthy, seasoned traveler?

The rough rumbling was replaced with the whoosh of air as the wheels left the tarmac. The man next to her quickly dropped his head into a slumber. Maddie was too excited to doze. She wanted to enjoy every moment of her premier, first-class flight.

I guess the stewards can't be walking around serving champagne during takeoff. But it would be nice—one last bit of all-inclusive luxury.

Maddie had a strong urge to write everything down—to capture the experiences, information, and prayers now that she had the chance. She glanced ruefully at her large sleeping neighbor. There was no way to reach her bag without waking him.

Guess I'll just enjoy the view.

She lay back against the airline seat and looked into the bright sky and the clouds below. Then, toward the front of the plane, she saw it. The most spectacular thing she'd ever seen.

Tubes of colored light, like something you'd see in a cartoon—red, orange, yellow, green, blue, indigo violet—ribbons were streaming across the sky. It was a vaporous rainbow like none she could have imagined, and the plane was going to cut right through. She bolted upright, pressing her forehead to the cabin window.

Oh my God, and there's another one—a double rainbow! The pilots must see it, too!

Her mouth fell open as she gaped at the incredible, vaporous tubes of color and light. Though she had seen many rainbows in her life, these were different. There was a marvelous otherworldly texture to them. She almost thought the plane might run into them instead of through them, like running into a clear glass window.

But I thought it was impossible to go through a rainbow—something about light refraction means you can only see rainbows from a distance. You can't be inside one.

She looked back through the rows to determine if everybody could see what was going on, but the other passengers were fast asleep. The excitement was entirely too much, and she couldn't help herself. She grabbed the hand of the man sitting next to her, a little too tightly, and cried out, "Look! It's a rainbow!"

The man lifted a heavy eyelid her direction, said, "Yah," and returned to his sleep—as if to say, "First time in first-class, eh?"

But Maddie Clare knew the sight was truly exceptional—and real. She leaned back and ran the experience through her mind over and over. The plane had sliced the rainbow in two, and incredible tubes of color had passed through her window.

She looked out to the sky again and caught her reflection in the glass—the young scribe, with dark brown eyes smiling, looked back at Maddie. She hoped this was a sign of peace in the matrix today. Looking through the reflection to the clouds below, the words from the early morning nap came back to her.

"Your life will be different now. More signs, symbols, and entities will come to you that reveal lost and forgotten truths. They come so they can be reignited on the grid for you and others to discover.

"You must remember being a scribe inside the temple, the scribe who promised to help the children. This promise will not be released. You must live the life that you were born to live. You will be protected, but you must also be prepared—for the next adventure, for the next knowing. In every lifetime you have been a keeper of universal secrets and truths, a scribe using different mediums. This life is no different. You must remember, Little One."

Maddie resolved to remember. And to share. And to prepare for the next adventure…

Not The End

THE
ADHERENT

EPILOGUE

Maddie put Maybelle outside and took a deep breath of anticipation as she headed up the stairs. She opened the closet door where it was tucked, safely on the shelf, still wrapped in the paper of Doña Rosita. The experience still seemed surreal. Everything about it was so otherworldly. The sacred altar piece that had been given to her so graciously by the Maya priestess, the conversation with Melchizedek, the fact that she had been inside the pyramid of El Castillo, in a room that hadn't yet been discovered.

With trepidation, she picked up the paper-wrapped Grandfather Manik and carried it to the living room. She had lit a white, vanilla-scented candle for the unwrapping. She felt it was only right to do *something* ceremonial since he'd been hidden away for a week.

Holding it gingerly, she curled up in her comfy chair. Then she held the package to her chest. She wanted to breathe with it a minute before she unwrapped it. She had no idea what to expect, with this Maya "altar-piece" in her home.

What have I done? You must feed it once in a while? I have no idea what do with an altar-piece from the Yucatec Maya.

Will it bring more entities like B'atz into my home? Will I begin having nightmares like I did before? Will it speak to me in the night? Bring Melchizedek? Or other apparitions? Or even stronger messages and visions?

There's no way to know. I feel I may have brought home a false god to pray to. How would I ever explain this to my dad? Or to a priest—a Catholic *priest?*

Maddie's fingers searched for a piece of tape in the wrap, so as not to tear it. Instead, her hands revealed a raised wax seal. As she turned it for closer inspection, she noted the wax was red, with a few errant drops on the paper. The letters, MCO were clearly inscribed in the center.

That's not right. I would have certainly seen her stamping this. Once she showed me the statue, she didn't take it out of my sight again. How in the world could it have my initials stamped in it?

Sliding her finger under the seal, she slowly peeled back the layers. For a moment, she wondered if something might happen, if something other than Grandfather Manik might be inside. She was relieved to see the unfired sculpture she remembered so clearly. She lifted it up to examine it more closely.

No damage. Whew! That's good. Made it all the way through customs, eh?

Okay Maddie. It's weird you're talking to it. Or even thinking about talking to it.

Maddie's chuckle cleared the tension of the moment. She set the piece down on the coffee table and returned her attention to the wrap. Spreading it out, she spotted some scrawled words.

Oops. I hope this wasn't her grocery list.

Again, she waved-off the heaviness of the moment.

Maddie turned up the light and donned her reading glasses. "Now you will know, my dear child."

What? What will I know? Are you kidding?

There was no answer. No voice of the gods. No voice of Grandfather Manik.

Now what?

In truth, Maddie did know. She reached under the chair for her journal, which hadn't been touched since the night she got home from Cancun. Her automatic writing had never failed her.

Whenever she sat with half-closed eyes and asked for guidance, her hand had taken the dictation of the Universe, scribbling and scrawling along the paper, leaving her with filled pages, of unknown content. It was only after the last words that she could turn back to the first page to read the message, which often had a pronounced prophetic tone. Sometimes symbols and diagrams and charts filled the pages that she could no more understand than if she'd seen them scribbled on a blackboard by some scientist at the University.

She'd been a little bit afraid to ask more and too leery to know the full story of what lie ahead in her life. Now it was time.

Taking a deep breath, she opened the notebook to the bottom of the last entry, where she would begin. Then she whispered the prayer aloud.

"Great Spirit. Guide me in my thoughts, words, actions and intentions this day. Heal me of any fear-based thoughts and bring your greatest and clearest direction to me. Give me clarity and light in doing that which is meant to be done by me. Allow me to see and receive messages that I may best serve myself and others for the highest good of all. Amen."

"My Dear and Loving Angels and Guides, speak to me as you will … of my time in Cancun, of this grandfather, of the message that Doña Rosita wanted me to know …"

With her eyes half closed, she let her pen move swiftly across the page as the words came into her mind, without pause or thought. There was only the sound of the pen scratching across the paper, moving lightly, with an occasional punctuation tap.

Though Maddie may have recognized that the words were that of a woman, her mind was not actively engaged, as it never was during automatic writing sessions. Like a translator, too busy converting the words to consider the context, Maddie soon found herself at the end of four pages loosely scrawled in her journal.

She sat with her eyes closed a moment longer, breathing softly and peacefully, confident that the answer she needed was already on the paper. Only then did she gently welcome her conscious mind to the present moment, to consider whose voice she had been transcribing. It had been the voice of the woman from the temple, the Keeper of the Universe.

Maybelle's bark jolted Maddie Clare back to her real-world living room, bathed in vanilla fragrance. She looked down at the words she had just scribed in inscrutable handwriting. She glanced to the window. Thankfully, Maybelle's bark had been that of playtime, not an urging for her to open the door. She was anxious to read the words for herself. She never knew what she had scribed, until she read it afterward. Swinging her legs over the comfy chair, she set her head back against the colorful upholstery and settled in to read the words of her destiny.

"Our dear Little One, we have waited to hear from you with love and appreciation. We know how overwhelming this shift in your life has been. Know that you are embraced and supported.

Yes, Dear One. You are one of the two, who will keep the promise. Of that, there is no question. Your heart is strong and loving and you will bring great guidance and tools to children through your books and words. Your very presence. Do not fear, you can make this "turning of the ship," this lifestyle change, in any way, timing, or manner that feels right for you. You have had a glimpse of the Divine Wheelhouse of the Illumination Station and you know it is nothing to be frightened of, only a way to change your role, your presence during this lifetime. We applaud you for your willingness to remember and to begin to scribe once more, as you did in your Maya life ... taking down the sacred messages of the universe.

You were correct in your suspicions of the priest. Though he grew up as a spiritual child, like yourself, some parts of his upbringing took him to a different path than the one he started. His soul thread carried too much memory of his time as one of the Gatherers, and his resentment at not being chosen to become a scribe like yourself. That angst pushed him to make other choices in this lifetime.

He has made it his mission to find the scrolls and the codex, for the current-day power they would give him in his role as a religious leader and a leader in Maya cosmology. While this is unfortunate, it is not yet set in stone. He has time to have revelations of his own, and therefore we must place him in prayer for his highest good, and the good of all.

Doña Rosita is also keeping that promise. Though you did not recognize her, she was the head priest, in your days as Naats' sayab, the young scribe.

You and Renato Martinez had known the head priest when you were all children. The three of you had run from the mud people in terror when they came for you in the corn fields of your parents, during the Blue Snake Cloud Ceremony. That day, because there had been so many children in the fields, many children were sacrificed. As you ran, all three of you separately had the same fervent prayer, to come back to save children from experiencing the darkness of terror.

All three of you managed to escape the grasp of the Gatherers, but only five could be chosen to join the sacred life as a scribe. It was not in the priest's journey in that lifetime, to carry the torch—through the pen of a scribe. For many reasons, unnecessary now, his task was to live as a Gatherer. He had opportunity then to save the children and did not ... and he has thus far turned from the pathway of protector yet again ... so far.

You saved the codex and the scrolls. They will be revealed in the right time, in the right manner. This is not to be your focus. Simply know that we are eternally grateful that you fulfilled your role in that lifetime to preserve the sacred truths.

And now, you come to understand the true meaning behind "eternally grateful"—a thread that carries forward through millennia.

The grandfather sculpture, which Doña Rosita gave to you, carries no burden with it. It was given as a gift of love and appreciation. Manik brings to you the opportunity to embrace self-respect. To remember the soul-memory you carry within you. This respect must be free of the influence of others so that you can heed the calling of your mission to teach the children the universal truths so that they may protect themselves. Manik watches over you in your travels, which will come soon, should you choose.

In fact, this was part of the final message you recalled from your days in the temple, transcribing the final codex. As the years of evolution have passed on the Maya calendar, we are nearing the top tier of technology. What has gone unnoticed is the inherent gift of the children to reach the Octaves, to understand and interpret frequency and vibration. These gifts will include telepathy, energetic healing, telekinesis, and the ability to bend the light once again.

You are more than you think, more than your conscious memory remembers in this moment. You have been a scribe in lifetimes past, taking down sacred truths from many cultures and spiritual practices. That soul-thread is still within you, still accessible. Have no fear. Embrace your purpose.

OTHER WORKS BY AMY GILLESPIE

Six Years in Mozambique:
Things I Haven't Told Mom

Available on Amazon.com and AmyGillespie.com

With its sweeping honesty, Six Years in Mozambique is the portrayal of an everyday life turned extraordinary when a purposeful heart overcomes. This is the story of change—the change that happens to you and because of you. Feeling a pulse on every page, it is the heartbeat of determination that tells the story of where real life meets the world according to Africa.

With $150 and the believe that all children should be given the skills to keep themselves and their loved ones alive, Amy Gillespie set out for Mozambique to meet the Goliath who had whispered to her in the night, "Come find me."

She could not have imagined all that she would witness and experience on her journey ... beauty, inspiration, humor; as well as corruption, unimaginable suffering, and shadowy threats from unlikely sources.

Six Years in Mozambique explores one woman's experience of the gritty reality of aid work, sexuality, and spirituality in Sub-Saharan Africa. It takes a raw look at what it's like to be a single woman, on the edge of forty years of age, setting off to chase down Goliath, with a raised sword, fully certain of success; and how that incredible journey led her to universal truths and surrender.

CPSIA information can be obtained
at www.ICGtesting.com
Printed in the USA
LVHW03s1437200618
581384LV00001B/99/P